Erotic Quill Publishing, LLC
3020 NE 41st Terrace STE 9 #243
Homestead, Fl. 33033
www.carmenrosales.com

First Edition

Manufactured in the United States of America First Edition November 2024

Hillside Kings Series
Hidden Scars
Hidden Lies
Hidden Secrets
Hidden Truths
Cartel Kings
Cartel Kings Book One
Steamy Romance Standalone's
The Sweat Box
Until Us
Love or Honor
The Prey Series
Thirst
Lust
Appetite
Forgive Me For I Have Sinned
Forbidden Flesh
Dark Romance
Dirty little Secrets
Sugar Coated Secrets
Like A Moth To A Flame
Giselle
Writing as Delilah Croww
Horror X
Whispers in the Dark
Circle of Freaks

Love is never silent

CARMEN ROSALES

The fight for love is the toughest match, and only the brave dare to enter the ring.

Ari

I ran from my past and hoped for a fresh start. I was desperate —I still am.

When I land a job at a boxing gym, everything seems to fall into place—until I meet Rey Vicente, known in the boxing ring as "The Silent King."

He's also my boss, off-limits, and hasn't spoken to me since I met him.

Every day I'm there, I find myself inexplicably drawn to the boxer. He's quiet, attractive, and brimming with muscle and power. I know how dangerous it could be to fall for someone like him, yet I can't get him out of my head.

The tension escalates every single day.

I watch him.

He ignores me.

He stares at me.

I look away.

The only thing more dangerous than falling is resisting.

The Sweat Box

CARMEN ROSALES

ARI

PULLING into the driveway of the townhouse, I place the car in park, ignoring the annoying whine of the timing belt as the car shuts off. I need to get that fixed. Hell, I need a whole new car. But with no job and only two hundred bucks in my savings account, I'm stuck with this beat-up Honda Accord caked with rust until I finish school.

I spot Jimmy's late-model silver Porsche parked in his space. I check the date and time on my phone to make sure I didn't miss anything. He should be at practice.

After I graduated from high school, it all happened fast. My parents followed me to Penn State to make sure I made it to my dorm building the weekend before college started. By the following week, I was dating Jimmy.

He was a popular freshman because he played hockey. Everyone knew who Jimmy was. He was the kind of guy you knew was in the room as soon as you walked in. Guys wanted to be him, and girls wanted him. He had the guy-next-door vibe mixed with the bad-boy look. His eyes are the color of moss, and he is tall with an athletic frame, brown hair, and a nice smile. I felt lucky the night he walked up to me and asked to hang out.

Back home, my parents were overprotective. I wasn't the popular girl guys gave a second thought about because I wasn't allowed to go out on dates. My parents only allowed girls to come over and only when they were home. I was embarrassed and always turned down anyone who asked.

When I unlock the front door, the blast of cold air from the air conditioner cools my heated skin. I scan the cream-colored couches in the living room.

After three years of living together, I find it weird that he isn't plopped on the couch watching TV.

"Hello," I call out. There's no response.

I notice the couch pillows are still in the same place I left them yesterday when I cleaned up. No dirty plates or cups litter the glass coffee table. He leaves a mess when he hangs out in the living room after he gets home from practice.

I place my handbag and keys on the table before heading up the wood stairs. When I reach the landing before the master bedroom, I smile, hoping I catch him taking a nap so I can crawl in, curl my limbs around his, and feel his warmth.

Pushing the door open, I hear the shower running from the en suite bathroom. The thought of him under the spray causes butterflies to swarm in my stomach in anticipation of joining him. I hope he doesn't mind.

"Babe?" I call out.

The water stops running. A muffled noise comes from the bathroom, and the door opens.

Water drips from his brown hair down his chiseled chest and abs and disappears in the towel wrapped around his waist.

My smile dies a quick death along with my voice. The rapid beat from my chest pounds in my ears. It feels like I've been gut-punched. Behind him is a naked blonde frantically trying to cover herself with a robe—my robe.

"A-Ari...I—" he stutters.

My hand covers my mouth as I try to keep my chin from trembling. Promises and panic mingle with my tears. I can't even think of the right words to say. It's like I'm not even in my body. Do I scream? Do I cry? Do I ask why?

Letting the wave of hurt rush over me while trying to contain the tears threatening to spill, I close my eyes briefly. I remember him introducing me to her three months ago as his friend's date. Her name is Mandy.

My eyes cut to her, and I let the truth sink deep with my eyes wide open. My self-esteem plummets even more with the way my favorite robe does nothing to contain the swell of her perfect breasts that are wet, ruining the silk material. I shouldn't compare, but I do.

Her perfect body.

How pretty she looks fresh out of the shower, freshly fucked, and how he did that. He made her feel beautiful and allowed her to use my things like it didn't matter—like I didn't matter.

"Look, I can explain," Jimmy says, holding his hands up.

Classy.

So fucking cliché, Jimmy. The next thing he's going to say is that he loves me.

I move to leave but then whirl around to face them. "Please, baby…" He pauses, looks nervously at Mandy with an expression of guilt, looks back at me, and continues, "It was just sex."

"Why?" I say in a shaky voice. "J-J…" I can't say his name. I can't—

"I'm going to leave," Mandy says, trying to tie the robe in a lame attempt to cover herself. She thinks she has a right to wear my robe after getting caught. She knows I'm with Jimmy and that we live together.

It's the last straw when I see her step to the side, and the scent of my body wash floats in the air. She's acting like she has a right to my things—to all I have. That she can leave like she isn't part of the reason my heart feels like it has been ripped out of my chest.

Besides the heartbreak of Jimmy betraying me, my pride kicks in somewhere deep in the pit of my stomach. I push back the sting from my eyes. The needles prick my throat.

"No," I tell her, finding my voice. "I'm leaving." I glance at Jimmy and then back at her. "He's all yours."

I march toward the closet and open the white closet door with more force than necessary, not caring that the handle dents the drywall.

"Don't go, Ari," he says in a calm voice. "I care about you."

"Oh... I can tell, Jimmy," I say while I hop up to grab my suitcase by the handle and pull it off the top shelf.

The good thing about being broke is that I don't have much to pack. We're over. Nothing he can say will erase the image of them together in my head. I won't believe anything he says. His words won't fix this.

I walk around the room, grabbing my stuff, pushing all his shit to the floor, regretting every time I've cleaned up after him. I pull the drawer open, swipe up all my clothes, and stuff them in my suitcase. I'm glad I only need to pack two drawers and a small amount of clothes in the closet, plus six pairs of shoes and my toiletries in the bathroom.

"I've known her since high school," Jimmy explains as if that makes fucking her behind my back a good enough reason.

I pause when I'm done with my clothes and shoes. Do I really need the stuff in the bathroom?

I'd have to walk in there, the place where my boyfriend just fucked another girl. Appalled and disgusted, I glance at the bed, blinking back the sting from the single tear that escapes, feeling like I'm being repeatedly stabbed.

I swallow hard, allowing anger to surface. "Then you should have asked Mandy to move in with you. You didn't have to lie, Jimmy. I could have just stayed in the dorm. We could have stayed friends, but no, you told me you loved me and wanted me to move in with you so we could always be together."

"You're not leaving," he says in a hard tone. Is he high?

I look up after flipping my suitcase closed, ignoring his last statement. "And I believed you."

I have two options. Leave my shit in the bathroom and come back later, or I can go to the dollar store, buy cheap replacements that make my hair stiff and dry my skin like I rubbed chalk all over it. I also won't have a flat iron or a blow dryer.

It takes me a split second to make my decision. The dollar store it is.

This is the story of my life, and Jimmy just shit all over it.

I'm broke.

I need a job.

I'm ten seconds from being homeless.

But I'd rather sleep in my car and eat gas station hot dogs than stay here and look at his smug face.

"Ari, is it?" I whirl around. What irritates me the most is that she acts like she doesn't know who I am. "I'm really sorry," she says apologetically. "You can have your robe back." She grabs her clothes from her back near the night- stand to go change in the bathroom like she owns the place.

Jimmy's eyes fall to her ass.

"You can keep it," I shoot back before she shuts the door and turns to leave.

Jimmy blocks my path. His eyes dip to my hand, clutching my suitcase. "You're not going anywhere, Ari."

"Fuck you," I say snidely.

He straightens to his full height. I'm amazed his towel is still wrapped around his waist. I try to shove past his hard body with my heavy suitcase, but he catches me by surprise and shoves me hard.

I fall, banging my shoulder against the solid wood dresser. Pain stabs my shoulder. My eyes widen. Fear slices through me at the anger filled in his green eyes.

"I don't think you heard me, Ari," he says evenly. "You're overreacting."

"I'm not! You pushed..." I scoot on the carpet toward the door when he steps closer, his fists clenched.

His eyes swing to the closed bathroom door and back. Then he lowers his voice. "You need to calm down. You're not leaving me. Put the suitcase back."

"No."

"If you don't"—he swallows—"I can't guarantee what will happen next." I'm shocked, stunned by the mad glint in his eyes. It makes my blood turn cold—the way his face sets and his eyes dilate. I can see the dark irises surrounded by moss green.

He takes another step, and my stomach swells with fear. The bathroom door swings open, and it's my only chance. He turns toward Mandy. Tears fall unchecked down my cheeks as I get up. Pain radiates down my arm, but I push through it. I grab my suitcase and drag it down the stairs, not caring if I dent the walls as I take each step.

"Come back here, Ari! I'm not finished with you," he yells.

Adrenaline spreads like fire. Blood is pumping in my ears when I reach the first floor. I grab my cell phone and keys and manage to pull the front door open like I'm running from a masked murderer in a slasher flick. The bright sun causes me to squint. Black spots appear like black-and-red butterflies, clouding my vision.

When I reach my car, I'm out of breath. My lungs are on fire. My heart pounds in my chest. My hands tremble when I fumble with the key to unlock the car. I blink rapidly, trying to adjust to the harsh light. My shoulder screams in pain when I toss my suitcase in the back. I slide in the driver's seat, shut the door, and power up my piece of crap Honda, ignoring the cry of the timing belt. I back out of the driveway, hearing the tires scream between my sobs as I peel out, not caring which way I go as long as it's away from Jimmy.

REY

MY PHONE BUZZES in my pocket as I push the door open from the medical center. I take it out, knowing it's my brother, Javier. He offered to take me to the doctor before heading to the boxing gym.

> Javier: What did the doctor say?

> Rey: What do you think? It's getting worse.

I pocket my phone when I open the passenger door of his truck, hop in, and stare straight ahead. He knows I no longer want to talk about it if I don't give him good news.

I scroll through my phone and create a new playlist of every song I like, organizing them by genre and workout days. On the way to the gym, it gives me something to do and keeps my brother from prying into my feelings.

From the corner of my eye, I watch my brother tap his fingers on the steering wheel, but I ignore him as I tap each song, building my playlist. He knows there is nothing to say. Nothing anyone can do. I don't even know why I bother going.

After twenty minutes of tense silence, he pulls into our gym's parking lot. I take my time getting out of the truck, allowing him to walk ahead.

I close the passenger door and fill my lungs with fresh air, giving myself a minute before stepping inside to get ready for the beating I'll give my body to get my aggression under control.

Boxing is what I'm good at. It's the only thing I know. It's my therapy. The way I learn to cope when life throws shit you can do nothing about.

Boxing has been everything growing up. Some boys have fathers, and some have stepfathers. Some have a father figure to look up to who understand what they're going through. Me, I had no one. It's not because I'm difficult. It's because they will never know what it is like to be me.

When I get punched in the face, it hurts like hell, but I get back up, learn from it, and fight back. It is the best lesson any father can teach their son. I learned that lesson through pain. I learned that lesson in boxing.

After changing my workout clothes, I leave the locker room and nod to guys already training as I pass. I make a detour to the office, where I find my brother pushing papers around in frustration. The dust motes float in the light from the sun streaming through the window as he picks up the messy stack of sign-ups for the new members who joined the gym last week. I take a seat.

He gets up, shuts the door, and twists the rod to close the blinds. He walks around me and sits in the chair behind the desk. He grabs a stapler to fasten four papers together, places them on the desk, and slides them forward.

I lean over the desk, read the heading, and roll my eyes when I see it's a job application. He grabs three sheets of paper where each paper is cut evenly at the bottom and moves like strings from a piñata. The gym's phone number is printed on each strip so it can be pulled off. He could have posted it online for job seekers on one of those websites, but this way is still effective. He wouldn't post it without my consent because he cares how I feel and wouldn't do anything behind my back since we're business partners.

He looks up at me, waiting for me to give him the go-ahead. Instead, I ignore him, walk out, and slam the door behind me. When I reach the punching bag, my phone vibrates before I place it on the bench.

> Javier: Avoid it all you want, but we need to hire someone.

Rey: No.

> Javier: Why?

Rey: It was supposed to be the two of us. You and me. That's it. I don't want to babysit someone while I train and run the gym. You know how I feel about bringing people into our business.

> Javier: Come back to the office. Let's talk about it.

I close my eyes, not wanting to talk about this now. Not now. My head begins to pound, and I can feel the vein in my temple throb. My phone vibrates again, and I glance at the screen.

> Javier: Come on, Rey. I need you to train me, and the office looks like shit. You can't do both. I won't have time to help you train the other fighters in my downtime, and you know it.

He has a point. We don't have much time to get him ready. We are also obligated to the other fighters who have paid good money to train in our camp.

Rey: Fine.

It's not like I can interview people.

After a minute, the throbbing stops, and I refocus. My phone vibrates again. I glance at it before I place it on the bench to begin my workout.

> Javier: I promise to hire the best person I can find. No te preocupes.

When he speaks Spanish, he reminds me of our mother. When we moved to the States from Puerto Rico, she would leave me notes written in Spanish to calm me down—a reminder of my childhood and where I came from.

Javier says not to worry, but that is exactly what I do when I place my headphones over my ears and begin to hit the speed bag after I press play. The faint beat of the music keeps me from losing my mind, though the worry spreads inside me. Who would he hire on short notice? Where does he plan to find this person? Can they be trusted?

ARI

THE GUY on the phone from the school's housing department comes back on the line. "I'm sorry, but no dorms are available, and there is a waiting list." Great, my worst fear has materialized. No dorms are available, and they are not even free.

I lay my head back on the headrest, wanting to drive back and punch Jimmy in the face. But then the fear of what he might do if he sees me returns. The look of anger clouded his eyes when he pushed me because I was leaving him. I wish I had time to figure things out. I would have preferred the dreaded "I want to see other people" speech than finding out the way I did.

"Alright, put my name down. If there are any cancellations, please call me right away."

"Will do," he says and hangs up. I moan in defeat. He didn't even ask me for my name or phone number.

Last night, after driving for hours not knowing where to go when I left Jimmy's house, I parked under a tree in the lot at a local park and cried my eyes out, feeling sorry for myself. I replayed what happened in my mind countless times. What he said. She acted sorry, but I knew it was a lie. People only say sorry when they get caught. If she didn't know about me, that is one thing, but she did. They both knew what they were doing, and they didn't give a shit about it. The way he shoved me without a second thought. I didn't mean to push past him, but he blocked the door when I tried to leave.

I tried to find blame within myself, to think about what I could have done differently to prevent him from doing what he did, but I found nothing.

After another two hours of crying, the hate for being naive kicks in. I should have never moved in with Jimmy. I wouldn't be sitting in my car in a parking lot with nowhere to go and no money to get there.

After three years of dating and many arguments with my parents, Jimmy convinced me to move in with him. I ignored all their warnings about me moving too fast and giving up my spot in the dorm on campus.

I should have listened to my parents. I should have listened to my gut instinct. I felt it the first month. I ignored the signs when he would watch TV, play video games, sleep, and not help me around the house when I was cleaning after him, but I wanted to prove to everyone that I made the right decision, especially my parents. They always thought I was incapable of doing things on my own, sheltering me when I didn't want to be sheltered.

Now I know why he didn't want me to pitch in for rent. He manipulated me so I would feel like I owed him. I hated that he was a slob, but I did love him. The worst part was I thought he loved me back. He ended up being a lying, two-timing piece of shit bastard.

My phone goes off for the eighth time since I called the school. Eight missed calls. I had to place it on silent last night to fall asleep. He's called me twelve times since I left the house.

When my voicemail was full, he resorted to texting me. The messages started out apologetic—he was sorry and wanted me to return home. Then they got demanding— angrier. Like I better get home now or I'll be sorry. And you can't run away from me.

I glance at my screen.

Jimmy: You're not leaving me. I love you.

He's delusional.

He must be out of his mind.

I think the cold and too many hits playing hockey have affected his brain cells. He pushed me, threatened me, and fucking slept with someone else. There is no way I'll consider going back to him. I can't even stand the thought of going back there. Just thinking about it makes me sick. Remembering the look in his eyes before I left was terrifying. It was a glimpse of what he would do if I stayed.

We're over.

I look down at the same clothes I was wearing from yesterday. My eyes cut to the wet spot on my thigh. I'm so tired. I haven't slept and would kill for a warm bed and a hot shower.

I pull the visor down to look in the mirror and see the dark circles under my eyes. I wipe my face with the back of my hand. "Come on, Ari." I sniff. "Get it together."

My fingers find the key in the ignition, turn the car on, hear the time belt screech, and wait for the warm air from the vents to hit my skin. I had to turn the car off to save gas because, right now, every penny counts. The temperature dips when the sun decreases as the fall season moves in.

During the day, it gets hot. My air conditioner doesn't work, but the heater does.

Jimmy promised to check it out or at least find someone affordable to fix it, but of course, like everything he says, it was a lie. He couldn't care less if I sweat like a pig during the summer months or freeze my ass in the winter. He preferred me to drive his car, but he insisted on being in the passenger seat to make sure I didn't put a scratch on it.

At first, I thought it was cute that he let me drive his car, but now I realize it's because he didn't want to drive. I dodged a bullet. My car makes a rattling sound like it can read my thoughts, warning me it's on its last leg, but thankfully, it doesn't quit on me. That would be the worst thing that could happen right now. To be on foot like a hitchhiker rolling my suitcase in the middle of the night on the side of the road with my thumb sticking out, looking for a ride.

My thumb swipes across the screen, ignoring Jimmy's text. I thought of calling my parents, but I couldn't tell them what happened because no one likes the "This is what you get for not listening to your parents" speech. I also can't show up there and ask for money they don't have because they will know something bad happened. Parents have a sixth sense about these things.

My parents are not wealthy and practically work paycheck to paycheck. If they discover the truth, they will make me withdraw from school, and I could kiss my future goodbye. I'd end up getting a job at Subway and living with my parents until I'm forty. I have to figure this out on my own. The first step is finding a job.

———

I find the cheapest drive-through and order from the dollar menu. I decided to eat early before finding a spot to park my car and call it a night. I have a big day tomorrow. I also can't risk using the bathroom at night when most places are closed and gas stations are notoriously full of weirdos. The bathrooms are always out of order, or they only have outside bathrooms, and you need to get a key from the cashier from the little drawer.

When I opened the door, my first thought was that there was a dead body inside when the putrid smell of shit and urine flooded my nose. I held my breath while I peed, stood, and almost passed out.

After the first night, I couldn't wait until morning to use the bathroom at the grocery store or fast food down the road when it opened.

After waking up feeling run over, I wipe the sleep from my eyes. The sun glares through the windshield. Large shadows loom as people walk on the paved pathway. Some are on their run. Their breaths form clouds from the cold.

When I move to sit up, my shoulder is stiff and sore. The painkillers I bought from the gas station yesterday have long worn off, but I manage to start my car, drawing glances from the people walking by when they hear the horrible noise.

At six thirty in the morning, I drive out of the parking lot before anyone calls the cops for violating the No Overnight Parking sign. My car draws too much attention, and I'm sure the same people I see at the park already know.

The dark circles under my eyes are darker when I look at myself in the rearview mirror. It seems like I was on the cast of *The Walking Dead*. My hair looks like straw. I tossed and turned the entire night. I woke up every two hours when the cold was too much and had to turn on the heat from the car. At around three o'clock, the fear of someone attacking me through the window set in. It was horrible. I didn't know how homeless people slept outside in the dark. How they weren't scared. I was grateful I had a car.

I turn left to catch the highway. One thing about the full-service gas station off the road is that no one cares how you look as long as you have clothes and shoes on.

Everyone looks like shit when they walk inside. Truck drivers look haggard from driving all night. Workers finished with their graveyard shift. People traveling across state lines needing to use the restroom.

After I freshen up in the accessible stall and make sure no one needs to use it, I pause when I look in the sink to brush my teeth. My stomach turns, thinking of all the germs floating inside, the string of hair at the bottom near the drain, and the smell of the water. I step back, brushing my teeth as fast as possible, trying not to think about it. After sipping from my water bottle, I rinse my mouth and spit in the trash.

After using the restroom, my determination to start my new job motivated me to overlook the bad and look forward to the good. The more I save, the less I need to find a restroom that doesn't look like fifty vagrants have used it before me.

I thought about using the restroom on campus, but the less I hang around, the less people notice me. Word has gotten around on social media that Jimmy and I broke up. The last thing I want is to run into someone he knew or, worse, him. I don't know how far he will go with his threats, but I don't want to find out.

I don't want people to know I'm vulnerable because I have no place to go. It would give Jimmy power over me to know I have nothing and no one. No friends. No money. I have already given him so much.

My trust. My heart. My firsts.

I refuse to give him any more pieces of me. I refuse to let him see how he broke me or that I'm scared of him. Deep down, I know he will hurt me if he finds me.

REY

"I HIRED SOMEONE," my brother says.

I take out my phone to text him instead since we're out on the floor and don't want people to eavesdrop on business matters.

> Rey: Quien?

> Javier: Una persona.

> Rey: Stop being funny, wiseass. I'm paying them. You could tell me who you hired and what you know about them. Hopefully, they won't steal from us or, worse, tell other camps our secrets.

It's not uncommon for people to hire spies to infiltrate other fighter camps. They can leak footage. That's why we train after hours and on Sundays when no one is scheduled to train at the gym. I'm undefeated and still have my title as the heavyweight champion.

My brother's upcoming fight has garnered much attention after he announced I'm training him. It also helps that he's outgoing, while I'm a mystery. I don't parade my wealth, and I don't interview.

After every fight, I thank the commentator and walk out of the ring.

Sure, I get paparazzi following me occasionally when I'm up for a fight. I'm not cocky or flashy. Nothing was handed to me. I've earned everything through boxing, including my mother's house and this boxing gym. I know what it's like to come from nothing, but I don't trust anyone who isn't my brother or mother.

> Javier: Relax. Don't worry, it's all good. I met the person yesterday. They will fill out the paperwork when they come in, and I'll run the background check to make sure they aren't a serial killer or a spy.

I grin.

> Rey: Esta bien. (Alright) I trust you. I'll give them a week. If they're not good, they're gone.

> Javier: Trust me. I have a good feeling about this.

———

The next day, after six hours of brutal training with my brother, I check the time on my phone. Right on cue, the glow from the afternoon sun grabs my attention as the front door to the gym opens.

A short woman, maybe in her early twenties, walks in with black leggings, a sweater sliding off one shoulder, and a pair of Vans. Movement in the gym stops. Heads turn. Before I can get a good look, she turns to close the door.

When she turns around, it feels like time has stopped. The earth has stopped spinning on its axis, disrupting everything.

My eyes slide slowly over her petite frame until they land

on a small nose, perfectly arched brows above dark lashes, and light brown hair in a loose ponytail that reaches her waist. She's gorgeous.

My eyes scan the gym, looking at the curious faces, probably wondering why she is here until I spot my brother leaning on the ropes in the ring's corner. He smiles and waves at her with his glove still on. Maybe, it's a girl he's dating, but I don't miss the tightness in my chest.

She returns his smile, and it gets worse. A lot worse. I take a deep breath, then look away and hit the speed bag harder to the beat of Eminem's "Till I Collapse." I hit the bag in a rhythm RIGHT-RIGHT- LEFT-LEFT.

My arms burn to their limit, and sweat stings my eyes. I stop, grab a towel, and wipe my face. I glance over and see a few guys huddled together, looking toward the office. David elbows Hector and gestures with his hands the way guys do whenever they notice an attractive woman. That is exactly why I made rules in the gym for all the fighters who sign up; no females or girlfriends are allowed in the gym unless they are parents or actual fighters. It causes too much drama and disrupts training. What if Javier saw them and lost his shit when he has a fight coming up? We can't have headaches like that in my gym.

The guys wait like dogs in heat until the office door opens. Hector bites his lip after David says something.

My blood boils. The same way it did when I was twelve and kids would bully me after school. The same way it did right before I landed the punch that would knock out my opponent. Hector notices me first, and his eyes widen. I can see his neck move as he swallows, dragging David down the small hallway to the locker room.

That's what I thought.

I pull out my cell phone and text my brother.

Rey: We need to talk.

Javier: What's wrong? ;)

He's being too nice. Either he knows I'm pissed off or worried I'm going to bitch him out.

Rey: Your girlfriend visiting the gym.

Javier: Que novia? I don't have a girlfriend, Rey.

Rey: Whatever, the girl you're dating. Don't invite her or any of them to the gym. It's distracting the guys, and they're talking about her.

Javier: Rey, I don't have a girlfriend, and I am not screwing anyone… at the moment. The woman you saw entering the gym is our new administrative assistant. Our new hire.

I look up at the aluminum ceiling of the massive warehouse and close my eyes for a second. Is he crazy? I wipe the sweat on my face with the towel, toss it on the bench, and storm my way to the office. Why in the hell did he hire her? Not that I have anything against women, but he can't be that dense. Is he blind? The guys' reactions as soon as she walked in are reason enough.

I open the door to the office. She is sitting in the chair—my chair behind the desk. Javier stands next to her, pointing at the stack of paperwork. He stops mid-sentence and looks up.

Her eyes land on me, igniting my blood. I stare directly at her, memorizing every part of her face. Every angle. Every curve. The color of her eyes, lips, and hair. The tip of her tongue when she nervously licks her lips. The tremble of her ringless fingers when Javier gives her the stack of unopened mail. My heart trembles. It stops. It begins. It turns, trying to understand why the rhythm isn't the same, but I know why. It's because of the woman in front of me and her strawberry scent.

She needs to leave.

Javier glances at me, and he can tell from the murderous glare I'm giving him that I don't approve.

I point at him, then at me, and nudge my head to the side, signaling we need to talk.

I enter the locker room, check each stall to make sure no one is inside, and walk back to find Javier with a tight expression.

He raises his hand. "What?"

"She needs to leave."

He gives me a stupid "I don't know what the fuck you're talking about" look.

I pinch the bridge of my nose to keep from losing my shit. I can't believe he doesn't see the problem with her working here. I love my younger brother, but he can be dense sometimes.

"Find someone else."

He shakes his head. "She needs the job."

"I don't care."

My heartbeat hasn't returned to its normal rhythm since I've looked at her. I can't think. I can't breathe, knowing she is still here.

"She is two semesters from graduating from Penn State with a degree in human resources. She's perfect."

"Tell her you changed your mind."

He slides his hand down his face in frustration. "Please tell me it's not because she's attractive."

I stare at him, not wanting to admit it. I don't want him to know how I'm feeling or what I think. With one look, she's managed to crack the iron wall I've built when it comes to the opposite sex.

"She doesn't belong here. This isn't a place for someone like her."

"You told me to find someone qualified, and I did. I don't have time for this. She stays unless she can't do the work. That is what you said, and I'm sticking to it. I won't tell her you don't want her here because she's too pretty. What kind of idiot says that?"

He's right. He needs to train for his upcoming fight, and we don't have time to find someone else.

"You deal with her. If someone gets out of line..."

"I'll deal with it like I always have," he says, then storms out.

I sit on the bench, hating myself. He thinks I don't trust his judgment when nothing is further from the truth. I blame it on my lack of interaction with people. I was never good at it, and once they found out the truth, I knew it would get worse. They would look at me differently. They would see how damaged I was. They would see my weakness.

ARI

THE MOST BEAUTIFUL man walks into the office with a venomous look in his eye while Javier shows me the membership sign-up papers, the requisite signatures for the waivers, and the dues that need to be collected.

I made the effort to give him my sweetest smile before introducing myself. I didn't know who he was, but I wanted to make a good first impression. I tried not to stare at how big he was. His frame filled the whole door, and his eyes were the color of warm chocolate under his cold stare. It didn't matter if he was rude or staring at me with cruelty on his gorgeous face. I want everyone to like me so they don't have a reason to fire me. I need this job to survive. I can do the work, but getting along with everyone is important.

When Javier informed me that he was his brother, my hands began to tremble. A tiny drop of sweat slid down my lower back. It meant he was also my boss. Unlike Javier, he wasn't overjoyed to have me here.

It's been ten minutes since Javier left after his brother. The dusty office looks like it hasn't been cleaned in over a year. A layer of dust coats everything. Documents and manila folders are strewn around the desk and on the floor, along with unopened mail from two months ago.

Behind me is a credenza that holds a dusty copy machine,

and stack of paper. Alongside the wall is a pile of brand-new T-shirts and sweaters with the gym's logo on the floor. Pens are scattered on the desk. The tape holder has a cloud of dust under the strip of clear tape. Paper clips litter the floor beneath the desk. Sticky notes hang on the computer screen. The office is a complete mess.

I take a breath and then let out a sharp cough. Dust floats off the keyboard from a late-model computer. A shame it's covered in dust. The trash in the corner overflows with wads of paper and plastic water bottles.

I spot a few picture frames of Javier and his brother wearing boxing gloves in a fighter's stance. The similarities are unmistakable, except his older brother is taller and bigger in build. Javier looks like a younger version of him. They both have a tan complexion, straight black hair shaved on the sides, a sharp jawline, and expressive eyes. They are both good-looking, but from what I've seen, they have different personalities.

Javier is laid-back and a lot of fun. His brother seems to be quiet and a complete jerk. The way he stared at me made my heart race. I became very self-conscious of how I looked. If I was wearing the right clothes for the job. If he could tell I hadn't slept from the dark circles I was trying to hide.

I get busy, not wanting them to think I don't lack initiative. The warehouse was converted into a boxing gym. The sounds of men's voices and fists striking bags echo off the walls. The odor is reminiscent of musty sweat and vinyl. I've never been to a boxing gym, but the office smells the same. It's only mingled with dust and paper. Maybe they wouldn't mind if I brought an air freshener after I cleaned it up.

Fifteen minutes later, Javier walks in, running his fingers through his hair.

"Is everything alright?" I ask.

He shuts the door, opens the blinds, and looks out the window. He places his hands on his hips for about a minute, like he is lost in thought.

After a few seconds, he turns around and sits in the chair in front of the desk.

"That was my brother."

"He seemed upset. Is everything okay?"

A look of unease crosses his face, and I notice he doesn't look me straight in the eye. A sick feeling turns in the pit of my stomach. Did I do something wrong?

I replay what happened since I walked in. I saw Javier, waved, smiled, followed him to the office, sat down, and waited for him to explain what to do next. He started off by giving me details on what was expected. Then his brother walked in, and I gave him a small smile. Introduced myself...

Javier clears his throat and scoots forward. He slides the sleeves of his hoodie up each forearm and begins to look for what I assume is the job application.

From what I've learned at school in my current program, it is customary for a new employee to fill out new hire forms and tax forms while providing identification and a social security card.

He lifts each stack of paper frustratingly, trying to find what he wants. I hand him the form I found after he left the room with his brother.

He lets out a sigh of relief and takes it.

"I already filled it out," I tell him, sliding my identification and social security card so he can make a copy. "Your brother doesn't approve of me being here, does he?"

He looks up after he scans the form. "Rey is...moody."

I lower my gaze. "Oh."

"Rey isn't used to needing help around the gym, and he has

a lot of pressure. Running the gym and training me for my upcoming fight. It's usually the other way around, me helping him out in the gym and him being the fighter."

I test his name in my head. Rey. I also don't see what Rey could be upset about. They agreed to hire someone, and I haven't done or said anything wrong. I get that some people are control freaks, but looking at this office, I hardly find that to be the case.

"When is your fight?"

"In twelve weeks. It is my pro debut."

My eyes widen, impressed. His first fight as a pro fighter. I thought he was just an amateur hoping to make it big. I don't follow boxing. When I was with Jimmy, hockey was the only sport I followed, and there wasn't room to watch or talk about any other sport.

"I'm sorry, but I'm not familiar with boxing. I mean, I get it. It is not that hard to figure out. You hit the other guy and avoid getting hit until you either knock him out or hit him enough times to win from how many punches you land."

He laughs. "I think it's a little more complicated than that, but that's basically the point. What sport do you follow?"

I sigh, not wanting to think about backstabbing Jimmy. It's what I changed his contact's name on my phone to yesterday after he wouldn't stop texting me to come home.

"Well, up until a couple of days ago, hockey."

I don't even like hockey that much. I watched the games and cheered for Jimmy because that is what a girl who loves her boyfriend does.

"Hockey?" He makes a face that tells me he isn't a fan. "You don't look like a girl into hockey."

I shrug. "My boy—ex-boyfriend is a hockey player."

A loud knock sounds on the door, and it is thrown open,

banging into the wall. Rey appears with that same pissed-off look on his face. Javier looks over his shoulder. Rey says nothing and gestures toward the door with his thumb so Javier can go with him.

To Rey, I don't exist. I'm not sure whether that is a good or bad thing.

AFTER I LEFT the locker room, I knew Javier went straight to the office to smooth things over with her.

I went back to the speed bag but couldn't concentrate. My eyes kept swinging to the office window, and I was glad he opened the blinds. I watched her grin at something he said. I wanted to yank him out of there by his shirt but went the safer route—training.

Javier is a good person. He has a way of making people feel at ease but couldn't help myself.

I can tell he is pissed that I barged in, pushing the door open, interrupting his conversation with our new employee by his hard stare. He knows not to make a scene in front of the guys. He needs to leave her to do the job she was hired to do.

Besides, what if she doesn't last the week? I'm a well-known fighter, and the last thing I need is a female selling a story on how she met Rey "The Silent King" Vicente to the tabloids for a payday.

Javier: Why did you open the door like that and tell me to leave the office? I don't start training until tomorrow.

> Rey: You were in there long enough. She can start organizing and cleaning the office before she starts the paperwork. Then she can deal with the merchandise. It will take her a week to get that place decent enough to start on the files anyway.

> Javier: You should introduce yourself. She's nice. I think she will be good for us. She already found the employee form and filled it out without me even telling her to do it. She took the initiative. It looks like she's had a rough couple of days.

A rough couple of days?

Javier pockets his phone, grabs a clear bag from the ice machine, and fills it with ice. He ties the knot and grabs a towel.

I pinch my brows in worry. Why does he need ice? Is he hurt? How did he get hurt when he hasn't trained today? I tap him on the shoulder and nudge my chin toward the bag of ice.

He holds out the bag. I take it while he places the towel over his shoulder. He slides his phone out and texts me.

My phone vibrates, and I hand him the bag of ice so I can take it out of my pocket.

> Javier: Relax, It's not for me. It's for her shoulder. She thought I didn't notice it bothered her when she handed me the paper.

I fired a quick text and almost regretted it. I shouldn't give a shit.

> Rey: How?

He shakes his head and texts me before grabbing the bag of ice and towel.

Javier: She didn't say.

———

Every weekday for the past week, I look at the time on my phone every fifteen minutes starting at 2:15. When it's finally three o'clock, the front door to the gym opens, and she walks in. Aria Jenson, but I've seen my brother call her Ari.

I looked at her file from the background check we had done on her. She was born and raised in Pennsylvania. She's an only child with a clean record and working-class parents. That's all I read. I could have hired someone to dig for more, but I didn't. Her personal life is none of my business.

When she shuts the door, I don't miss the way the guys stop to look for a second. She must be aware of the attention because she hurries toward the office. Right before she shuts the door, her eyes scan the gym until they find mine and every time, I look away.

I haven't introduced myself, nor do I feel the need to. She comes in on time, stays late, and handles the office. My brother convinced me to make her a key a couple of days ago so she could lock up. I'm not sure I like the idea of her being the last one to lock up on her own. It's not that I don't trust her, but I keep telling myself I care for her safety. But deep down, I know it's more than that.

ARI

I JOLT when I hear banging on the bathroom door, followed by a muffled, "Hey, get out of there."

I shut off the blow-dryer, quickly pull the cord from the electrical socket, put it in my bag, and tie up my hair.

I pull open the bathroom door and find the manager of Hardee's with a disapproving glare aimed my way.

"This isn't a salon. You homeless people need to go to a shelter and stop freeloading." I lower my head, avoiding her glare. "I'll give you one second to pack up your shit and get the hell out of here, or I'm calling the cops."

I step out, trying not to slip on the greasy brown tiles with my carry-on. Tears prick my eyes as people stare, watching me leave. When I'm finally inside my car, I let the tears fall.

I've never been kicked out before.

I've never been called homeless.

I needed to blow-dry my hair. I tried the athletic department locker room on campus, but they asked for ID and if I was an athlete to use the showers. My hair looks like shit, and people are starting to notice. I have until the end of next week to get my first paycheck from the gym. I can't leave my hair wet because it's getting cold out, and the last thing I want is to get sick.

When I turn the key to start the car, I jump when I hear a

bang on my driver's side window, causing my heart to beat so hard it feels like it leaped out of my chest.

I look over, and it's the Hardee's manager.

"Alright, I'm leaving!" I say loud enough so she could hear me.

"Open up," she says, tapping the window.

I roll the window an inch. "Look, I'm sorry—"

She slides a piece of paper through the crack of the window. "Here. It's the address and phone number of a shelter. It's dangerous to be doing what you're doing at this time of night." It is ten thirty at night. I take the piece of paper. "I'm sorry for being a bitch back there, but I'll get fired." I nod, knowing how important a job is when you need it. "Show up or give them a call. I don't know your situation, but it's better than being out here."

I blink back my tears and swallow the lump in my throat. "Thanks."

I call before driving and using my gas, but they're full for the night. They said to try again tomorrow but took my information. The lady said I could go to a fire station to pick up a hot meal, but I don't need food. I need a hot shower and a place to sleep.

———

It's Wednesday before they have a spot available at the shelter. It smells awful. I ignore the curious glances from women. Most of them were looking at my bag and shoes. They smell like shit and in need of a shower. They remind me of the gas station restrooms.

When I reach the end of the line with a hot plate, a lady with dark hair pulled back in a hair net behind the counter gives me a once-over. "Whatever you do, don't fall asleep," she warns.

"Why not?" I ask.

I look at the women sitting on the benches with plastic garbage bags with everything they own, watching me while they eat. Some have missing teeth. Others have spots on their skin from drug use. Matted hair.

I glance back at the older lady sitting next to the woman with the dark hair. They are both volunteers in purple shirts with the women's shelter logo embroidered on their left pocket.

The older woman leans forward, lowering her voice. "A pretty girl like you. You're fresh meat in a place like this."

"If you fall asleep, they'll steal your shit," the dark- haired lady adds.

I didn't sleep. Hell, how could I with a warning like that? I was grateful for the free food. They were right about people taking your things. Three women woke up in the morning with their bags stolen. They were crying, and all the shelter staff could do was give them clothes from the donation box. I feel bad for them, but I have nothing to offer them.

Staying at the shelter comes with a price. Not sleeping isn't an option.

In the morning, I look like a zombie. I'm running out of concealer and foundation. I have to figure out where to shower safely and take my chances sleeping in my car. I couldn't stay awake after three cups of coffee. I couldn't study or finish my homework.

When I walk into the gym at three o'clock for work, I don't bother to look at Rey. I would sneak glances when I could but right now, I'm dragging ass.

The man is a machine when he trains, his body a work of art. He is quiet. What I found weird compared to everyone in the gym was when people would try to talk to him, he ignored them. He doesn't have a conversation with anyone.

The few times Javier was around, they always went somewhere private. I found it weird. Weird enough that I googled him, and what I saw was a surprise. I work for the heavyweight champion of the world. I'm not going to lie and say I wasn't impressed. He's impressive.

They call him "The Silent King."

According to the articles I found online, he's single. It doesn't take a genius to know why he is unmarried. He is closed off and introverted. Lonely. Silent. He doesn't speak more than two words after a fight. He doesn't show off like other boxing champions and only cares about his brother and mother. His mother raised him in Puerto Rico before moving to the US when he went pro. There was no mention of a father.

When I got a closer look at him the first day, I saw something in his gaze. Beneath his cold stare was something warm. I felt safe when he looked at me like that, but frightened at the same time. I've never been looked at that way before.

When I walk through the gym's main floor, I avoid eye contact with the guys training, but I can feel the heat of Rey's stare when I fold the towels. I sneak a glance when he starts to hit the bag. He has a dangerous look in his eyes, and the thought of feeling safe quickly vanishes. The raw power of each blow he lands causes me to flinch. Each one lands harder than the last. His sweat drips like body oil down his muscles, disappearing in the ink drawn on his skin.

I don't think he's noticed me watching, but I can't tear my gaze away. He is behind the bag, his mouth making a hiss with each strike. A strand of dark, wet hair falls forward, followed by more sweat down his chiseled jaw. He's beautiful. Like a real-life Goliath. Beautiful from afar, dangerous up close.

I can hear the music coming from headphones. They must

have them turned all the up if I could make out the lyrics of Eminem's "The Way I Am."

He continues to work hard on the bag, and my eyes are transfixed on the way he moves his feet in his boxing shoes. My eyes slowly lift to his chest muscles, which look like oiled pistons as they bunch and vibrate.

When he looks up, I avert my eyes nervously, dropping the towel on the floor. A shudder runs through me as I bend to pick it up, fold it, and place it on the rack.

I jump when I realize he's right behind me. His gaze fixed on me. The intensity of his eyes when they ran all over me. Eminem's "Superman" lyrics mock me from his headphones.

I place the stack of folded towels from the basket on the rack, ignoring the way he made me feel naked, stripping me piece by piece. His hand reaches in to grab a towel. My breath hitches in my throat when the tip of his finger brushes lightly over the top of my hand before grabbing a towel. I snatch my hand away, rubbing the skin like I was burned by the tip of a burning flame. My pulse beats frantically in my throat.

My eyes lift. He slides the headphones off his head and wipes his face and chest, full of sweat over tan skin and tattoos. When he's done, I forget I'm watching him instead of working. I step back, but his icy stare pins me to the spot. He closes the distance between us.

"D-do you need me to take the towel?" I stammer, trying to think of the right thing to say, but he doesn't reply.

His gaze travels slowly over my face. Alarm bells ring in my ears, telling me to run while I still can, but I push it away. I lift my chin, waiting for him to tell me what he wants, what he needs, or what I've done, but he looks down at me, cutting me with his gaze like a knife. He takes the towel, places it in the empty basket, and walks away.

ARI

I COULDN'T STOP THINKING about Rey last night. I tossed and turned in my car's driver's seat, refusing to go to the shelter. I tried to forget how he looked at me but couldn't. Every time I closed my eyes, all I could see was his vicious stare taking a piece of me or the way he hit the punching bag like he was exercising a demon.

I grab the stack of unopened bills, toss the ones Javier already marked as trash, and pause when I see Rey's name. It's from a medical practice downtown. I turned it over and saw that it had already been opened. I look through the small window to see if Rey or Javier are still here from running errands, but it's just the three guys who were already here when I showed up and came in.

It's not my business to know his personal issues. It's wrong and most likely illegal to read them, but it's not like they were unopened. I know pro fighters can have concussions and get hurt like in any other sport, but Rey's different. He is a mystery. Very few people know him, and from what I've read on social media, there isn't much about his personal life.

I bite my bottom lip when I unfold the paper. It's a copy of a bill for three thousand dollars to a psychiatrist, psychotherapist, and specialist. The type of specialist is not listed.

"Hey."

I drop the paper with an envelope, and it floats away like a leaf in the breeze under the desk. I clear my throat as Javier walks in and takes a seat.

"Hey," I say with a nervous smile.

"I didn't mean to startle you."

"Oh, you didn't. I didn't realize you guys were back. I was lost in going through the mail."

"Yeah, Rey has an appointment, and I had to pick up some stuff before they closed for the day."

He glances at the stack I was going through. I didn't move to pick up Rey's medical bill because he would have seen that I opened it instead of placing it in their personal bin.

"Is everything alright?" I ask, hoping he will share something about his brother.

"Everything is good." But I don't miss the way his eyes dim a bit. "Did you guys eat?"

On my second day, they are training and doing drills with the new members who signed up and ask me to order them food from a health café.

"No time," he says, looking through the mail I placed in his bin.

My stomach growls. He pauses and looks up. "Hungry?" I shrink in my seat in embarrassment.

If I plan to get an apartment, I can only afford to eat one solid meal a day. In the morning, it's anything under three bucks. I eat again after I leave here for the day. If I'm lucky, I make it to the shelter and get a free meal, which helps me save on the cost of food.

"I'll eat later."

"How come you didn't get to eat?" he asks, concern etched in his voice.

"I had a test today," I lie. "I got out pretty late and came straight here."

"That sucks. What class was it?"

"Organization behavior."

"Sounds fancy."

"I guess."

"Want me to order you something?" He offers.

I shake my head. "That's okay. I can wait. I wouldn't want to get greasy marks on your mail."

He grins. "It's cool. I'm sure you're not the type to smear grease everywhere."

"I'm fine, really," I assure him when I see him pull out his phone.

"I can't have you passing out. What will it be? Let's see..." He scrolls through his phone. "All the places I can't eat. I want to live dangerously through you."

"Javier..."

"Pizza, Chinese, burgers," he says. "Oh...wait...Spanish." He rolls his eyes in ecstasy like he can taste the food. "I would kill for some rice and beans."

"It can wait. I swear."

I can't have him order me food when I don't have the money to pay for it. It would look bad when the delivery guy shows up expecting me to pay when all I have is one hundred and fifty bucks to my name. I need the money to wash clothes at the laundromat, buy food, and gas.

"Hm... I got it." He looks up like he didn't hear me with a mischievous look in his eyes, like he cracked the code to the vault. "Philly cheesesteak."

"Javier..."

He dials the number and places his phone to his ear. "Onion or no?"

"I don't...no..."

"No onions," he says through the phone.

Shit. I don't want to be rude and tell him not to order me food, but I can't. The last thing I want is to be at odds with

Javier when I need this job. It's bad enough that his brother hates that he hired me. I mentally calculate how much I have in my wallet, hoping it will be enough for a tip.

It would be cheaper to go and pick it up, but right when that thought crosses my mind, he hangs up and says, "It will be here in twenty minutes. Now that I know you have food, I gotta go condition with a couple of the guys."

After about twenty five minutes, I hear a knock on the door. A guy with a plastic back containing my food stands in the doorway. "Delivery for...Ari."

"Yes," I say, dreading spending the money I don't have for the food I desperately want to eat.

"Eighteen oh three," he says.

I rummage through my bag for the twenty-dollar bill, wishing I had more to give him for a tip.

"Oh, thanks," the delivery guy says in surprise. Confused, I look up and shift uncomfortably in my seat.

Rey towers over him, grabbing my food after handing the delivery guy a fifty-dollar bill. The guy digs in his pocket to give him change, but Rey dismisses him and turns around to face me. I swallow because he is shirtless. Sweat coats his beautiful skin from working out. His eyes drop to the money in my hand.

"Thank you." I reach out my hand to give him the money. "Here, for the food."

He doesn't take it. He doesn't say anything and places the food bag on my desk.

"Here is your change," the delivery guy says behind him. I forgot he was there. Rey shakes his head when the guy steps forward, trying to hand it to him, but his eyes are on me, watching me put the money away. "Thanks for the tip," the delivery guy says with a smile and walks out.

"You didn't have to pay for my lunch," I rush out even

though I'm relieved he did because I need it. Every penny counts.

He finally looks away and moves to where I placed the membership forms for everyone who has signed up for the gym in a separate pile from the ones who have made it to his camp.

He picks up the stack while I take the food. The smell fills my nose when I open it, and I almost groan at how delicious it smells, but I don't want him to know that I'm starving—literally.

"Is there anything you want me to do?" I ask him, but like always, he ignores me and continues to look through the pile with a determined expression.

After a few seconds, he pulls out two membership forms. It's the tenth of the month, the day I collect payment for memberships for the current month. I'm surprised when he places them in the cancellation bin and walks out, shutting the door.

I don't move. I'm confused that he went out of his way to pay for my food, and even more so when I pick up the forms and see the two members he wants me to cancel.

I read the stipulation on the form that states the owners and management have the right to cancel without cause at any given time. Hector Ramirez and David Rothstein.

REY

"WHY DID you cancel their memberships with the gym?"

"They didn't... work out."

"Not funny, Rey."

I shrug like it's no big deal, but to Javier, every fighter who wants to train and improve is a big deal.

"We are almost at capacity as it is. Someone will take their places by the end of the week."

"Fine. But I want to know why?" I glance toward the empty office.

"I thought they were good."

My eyes slide to his. "I have my reasons."

I don't wait for him to respond. I press play on my headphones. The faint beat from the music plays as I hit the speed bag. It's almost midnight. The gym is empty, and I know he will leave because he needs to be up at four in the morning for his run.

———

After Javier leaves, I head to the office and don't bother turning on the light before I sit behind the desk in the dark. I close my eyes and take a deep breath, inhaling the scent of strawberries.

"Your son has a problem with his anger, Mrs. Vicente. I understand he has a long road ahead, but we can't have this behavior in our school." I could still hear their muffled voices from where I sat outside the office.

"Please," my mother pleads, trying to hide her accent. The anxious look she gives the principal from Texas tears me apart inside. Mr. Gonzalez is originally from Puerto Rico and moved to the States after he was hired last year. "Rey is a very good boy," she continues. "He has a kind heart. What about the other kids? Did you speak to their parents about how they pick on my son?"

"We have. But we also had one kid with a busted nose and another one with a bruised jaw. Some witnesses say when he was provoked, he attacked them. One said it was because he was teased, and the other because of a girl." The girl wouldn't leave me alone and wanted to give me a blow job in the bathroom. She was pretty enough with dark hair and a pretty face. It also helped that she was Marcus's girlfriend. She was upset after I ignored her and then told Marcus I was a freak that left her alone.

"Violence is not tolerated," Mr. Gonzalez finishes saying. "They provoke him because he was placed in special classes. My son deserves to be treated the same."

"Mrs. Vicente, placing your son in a regular class will not help him. He has stopped speaking. He needs..."

"I know what my son needs. He needs to be treated like a normal thirteen-year-old boy."

I watched the principal's irritation cross his face. All I wanted to do was walk in there, reach over the desk, and show him what normal felt like, but I couldn't. I could see the strain in my mother's eyes—the dark circles from lack of sleep. I was the cause. I was the problem.

"He is...under the circumstances. We are willing to keep him here if he can behave like he is supposed to after a school psycholo-

gist evaluates him. If you could discuss this with his father, maybe he..."

"He left," she blurts. "Unfortunately."

The principal's face softens a fraction, and he says, "I see."

He didn't. No one saw, and no one cared. All they saw was a troubled teenager with a problem—a problem that would get worse.

I wake up with a jolt. I look around the dark office and realize I fell asleep in the chair. I sit up and rub my sore neck and stretch my stiff muscles.

Memories from my past remind me of what people thought of me. I'm considered violent, quiet, and emotionless. That was what they see when they looked at me—the part I let them see.

I never thought anyone would ever see the real me, that a person could simply didn't exist. That I would be doomed to ever feel anything other than guilt and anger. Guilt for my brother and mother for what I put them through. Anger for my father leaving and the way the rest of the world thought of me.

Some say angels exist, and for some, they have appeared. That's what crossed my mind after I saw her for the first time. That was what she looked like sitting in the chair. The way the sun hit her with the glow of its rays when our eyes first met— an angel with soft features and a soft nature—even the way she looked at me. If she only knew what I saw and how I felt, but I could never tell her. I have to keep her at a distance if I can't convince Javier to let her go.

I take a deep breath, and the scent of strawberries floats in the air, calming me the same way her smile does. The glint in her eyes when she talks to me, with her pink lips two shades away from red against her creamy skin. All I can do is watch her when she isn't aware and ignore her when she knows I'm around.

I don't care if she is frustrated. I don't care if she hates me for not wanting her here even though a part of me wants nothing more than for her to stay. I prefer her to hate me than to see the look in her eyes if she knew the truth.

MY STOMACH SINKS. My heart beats like a speeding train.

I scan the benches as soon as I leave the housing office. People must see the look on my face because they give me worried glances. My heartbeat returns to normal when I don't recognize Jimmy or one of his friends. There are times I think he will pop out of nowhere.

I have deduced that Jimmy can't take rejection very well. A guy like Jimmy isn't used to people telling him no. Ever since he went pro after a year of college, he is used to everyone doting on him, giving him whatever he wants and listening to everything he says. He is the two-time MVP for the Flyers. No one would believe me if I said he was violent.

He's called me incessantly, threatening me if I don't go back with him and won't leave me alone.

I rush to my car without attracting too much attention, walking through the throng of people in the afternoon rush to the pep rally. Penn State has a football game, so the campus is full of students preparing for the game.

When I reach my car, I let out a sigh of relief and turn it over, ignoring the stares as I put it in reverse, and it screams out of the parking lot.

> Jimmy: You can't do this to us. I love you, Ari. I'll prove it to you.

Please don't. Leave me alone.

The nights I've spent alone, wallowing in self-pity, I spend thinking about my relationship with Jimmy. I've started seeing things in a whole new light.

The selfish way he was with me when he had sex. It wasn't memorable, but I had nothing else to compare it to. It wasn't like I've read romance novels or seen posts from women on social media when they write about finding love. When I was with Jimmy, it wasn't explosive or heart-pounding. I was more self-conscious. Like I wasn't good enough. I didn't measure up to the other girls around him.

In a way, he made it seem like I was lucky to be with him. I remember the girls' smirks when we hung out with the other guys on the hockey team. They would look at him like they knew something I didn't.

It all makes sense, like puzzle pieces finding their way to where they belong, so I can see the full picture.

I was never beautiful in his eyes. I wasn't what he wanted. I was convenient. Someone stupid to believe his lies. The one who swallowed my doubts because I was afraid of being hurt. I was foolish and blindsided to have fallen for his shit. Who knows how long or how many people he has screwed behind my back. What he is capable of when he doesn't get what he wants with me.

I get to the gym after buying a water bottle at the sporting goods store. Javier had a spring water dispenser placed in the gym. I get thirsty at night in my car, and filling up the water bottle is more cost-effective than buying bottles of water. It is also a better option when I need to brush my teeth and rinse out my mouth.

A couple of guys are talking outside, blocking the door. A strong gust of wind blows the leaves against the building.

I spot Javier's truck and smile when I see Rey's black Range Rover parked beside his. I could give Rey the gift I bought him. It isn't much, but I hope he finds it useful. I want to thank him for paying for my lunch last week. He refuses to speak to me, but it's worth trying. I want to show him how grateful I am. It was the biggest meal I had, and I was able to save the rest for later so I didn't have to drive to the shelter that night.

Right before I walk inside, a guy steps in front of the door and holds it open. "Hey, you're the office girl," he says, running his gaze over me.

"Yeah," I say vaguely.

The guy next to him gives me a grin and then drops his gaze to my chest. I'm wearing a fitted black sweater with matching leggings, but it's like I'm wearing nothing in his eyes.

"I heard you're new," he says with a playful smirk, tilting his head to the side.

"Yes. I started two and a half weeks ago," I say with a polite smile as I step inside from the cold wind. "My name is Aria, but most people call me Ari."

The door shuts. "Let's go, man. We're going to be late," his friend says, pulling him by the hood of his sweater. "You know they won't think we're serious if we show up late for our workout. We still have to change."

But his friend ignores him and steps closer, snagging his bottom lip with his teeth. The way he keeps looking at me makes my skin crawl.

I feel heat on the side of my face. Like needles grazing my skin as I look away, wanting to get away from him.

He gives me one last run with his gaze, pausing between my legs and chest, and then slowly says, his lips carving in a nasty smile, "I'll see you around, Aria."

I walk away with my head down. When I get to the office, I shut the door. The thought of giving Rey his gift evaporates because I don't want to go back out there.

I sit behind my desk, placing the sporting goods bag near the keyboard. My lips curve into a smile when I see an origami swan neatly placed near the tube of strawberry lotion I left. I pick it up, carefully inspecting the expertly folded paper.

The door swings open, and Javier walks inside, out of breath. "Nice," he says to the swan in my hand. "Can you hand me the first-aid kit?"

I place the swan on the desk and quickly grab the first-aid kit bag behind me. "What happened?" I rush out, handing him the bag. "Is everything alright?"

He shakes his head. "My brother trains too hard sometimes."

It feels like a brick fell on my chest, imagining Rey hurt.

"Is Rey hurt?" I ask, getting up and wiping my nervous hands on my thighs. "What do you need me to do? Do I call for help?"

He lets out a deranged laugh. "Uh...no. It's the other guy. He's bleeding from his lip and eyebrow. I'm not sure if he needs stitches."

He grabs antiseptic, gauze, triple antibiotic ointment, and temporary strips. I feel useless and want to help.

"Tell me how I can help, Javier."

He grabs as many items as he can. I can hear loud voices coming from the ring in the center of the gym. "Grab some water and more gauze."

I grab what he needs and follow him out to the ring. I freeze when I see the blood pouring down the guy's face. He is sitting on a chair in the corner of the ring, and it's the same guy from earlier.

"You wanted to get in the ring with the champ," his friend says, shaking his head. "You can't roll with the big dog if you don't have the skills."

"I wasn't looking," he counters, trying to wipe the blood and sweat flowing like a river down the side of his face.

"Come on, Mike, admit it. He got you good, bro. There was no way you could have blocked him," he says in amazement. "He's fast, and when he hits, it's like a semi-truck moving like a freight train."

"If it makes you feel better, he's undefeated for a reason," another guy says behind him.

Mike is breathless; he blinks twice, trying to get the blood from going into his eye. "I don't know what the fuck is up with him. He doesn't go this hard. It was like I was an enemy," he says, looking at Javier. "What the hell got into him?"

When Javier steps into the ring, I can see Mike's skin split open about half an inch above his brow. The corner of his lip has a nasty cut. The whole left side of his face is swelling.

Javier kneels to clean him up. "Don't get in the ring with my brother if you don't have experience. He only has two sparring partners when he prepares for a fight." He looks directly at Mike. "Unless you did something to piss him off."

I walk up and move to hand the water bottle, but a tall shadow emerges, causing me to place it on the corner to look up.

Rey's chest heaves like a volcano, ready to erupt. I can see his ribs above his ab muscles contracting. Rising and falling with each heavy breath he takes. He pulls his gloves off with an angry snarl on his face aimed at me. I step back. He glances at Mike, and his lips curve in a malicious smile. I don't know how they don't see it. The satisfaction in his gaze for hurting Mike. It's probably why he is the best in the sport. But only a person with a black soul would smile like that after inflicting pain on someone.

I look away but can feel his gaze breathing fire against my skin.

"Ari, the bandage," Javier says with his hand out.

I fumble with the packet in my hand but manage to give it to him. After Javier patches up Mike the best he can, Mike tries to get up, but it takes three other guys to help him. I see bruises forming on the side of his ribs.

"What were you trying to do? Kill him," I mutter, stepping back so that they have room to get Mike out through the ropes.

"One would think?" a guy says, standing beside me with a towel around his face. "He looks pissed off, but no one will ever know what is going through his head except maybe his brother."

"Why is that?" I ask to know everything I can about the man who stole my thoughts.

"No one has heard him speak except two words after a main fight."

"Why?"

Rey is the last one to step out of the ring. He still has that hard look on his face when he passes me.

"No one knows," the guy says quietly. "He keeps to himself. I think it's dangerous."

"What is?" I ask, watching Rey walk to the locker room, throwing his boxing gloves by the bench near his headphones.

"To not know what he's thinking," he says in a low tone

like it's a big secret. "Every fighter that has gone in the ring with him doesn't know if he is angry or hates them."

"Do you think he is...crazy?"

I think back to the medical report he received in the mail, which I placed in his bin exactly as I found it.

"Angry and passionate, but I'm not sure about crazy. This doesn't happen. At least not since I joined six months ago when they first opened. I don't know what happened or if Mike pissed him off somehow. He said he didn't do anything but wanted to feel him out in the ring. To know what it's like to be in there with the best."

I guess he found out. But I don't say that.

After Javier drives Mike to the clinic to get checked out, I head to the office, trying to piece everything together. I think about what the guy said about Rey not speaking. Javier never mentioned it when he talked about Rey.

After three hours, I fill out an incident and injury report. The gym isn't liable since all members sign a waiver. I lean back and look at the gift I bought Rey.

I turn the rod from the blinds and see Rey in front of the mirror with a jump rope. At his speed, it looks like he is inside a portal traveling through time.

The gym is almost empty except for four guys lifting weights. I grab the shopping bag and pull out the sweatbands I picked up for his wrists. I hope he will like them. He can put them over the wrists of his gloves to wipe sweat from his eyes instead of having to take his gloves off to get a towel.

I keep a safe distance and wait until he spots me. He slows the rope down when I smile. He holds the ends of the jump rope in one hand and gives me a "what the hell do you want" look.

I bite my lip, step close, hold the sweatbands in my hand, and motion for him to remove his headphones. When he takes them off, he raises a brow, annoyed that I interrupted him.

His veins stand out over his forearms. His chest is chiseled. He looks strong and powerful. I swallow nervously. "I wanted to thank you for lunch the other day. Um, I got these for you." I hold them out to him. "So you wouldn't need to take off your gloves, or...when you're training, and the sweat gets too much, and you don't want to stop to get a towel."

I look up, but he doesn't look happy. It's like everything I just said didn't have meaning. His eyes bore into me while he grinds his teeth. He looks at the sweatbands, and then his gaze lifts. I could see myself in the storm of his chocolate depths. I didn't know why he looked so angry or why he was so cruel. Maybe I misjudged what I was giving him, and he found it mundane and stupid—a useless waste of his time.

There were plenty of times Jimmy hated it when I brought him something, only to find it in the trash or left forgotten on the couch. A shirt, something for hockey, a good luck charm. I didn't make the money he did, and maybe I never would, but I tried with the money I had left from school or the odd summer jobs I got to make extra money.

I thought Rey would like it. It isn't much, but how he looks at me tells me he doesn't. It was stupid to think he would bother liking it. A man like him doesn't need a pair of sweatbands from a homeless college girl he never wanted working in his gym in the first place.

After a few seconds, my stomach sinks. My chest feels like it was stabbed. He rolls his eyes and places his headphones back over his ears. He swings the jump rope, causing me to step back.

I drop my hand. "You hate it," I say quietly, even though he can't hear me through the loud music. "It was stupid."

I walk away, blinking back tears like a wound that wouldn't stop bleeding.

When I get to the office, I'm glad it's time to leave for the day. I grab my bag and hate myself for being naive. It's why my parents sheltered me so much all the time, or maybe it was their fault for sheltering me. I wasn't tough enough or smart enough to make the right choices.

I open my purse, pull out a desperately needed fifty- dollar bill, and drop it in Rey's bin. Grabbing a sticky note, I write For Ari's lunch and place it over the money and sweatbands. He could give them to someone who would appreciate it, but my pride won't let him win.

My eyes fall on the origami swan. Anger has me gripping it in my fingers and ripping it apart. It's stupid, maybe even juvenile, but it must have been him if it wasn't Javier who left it. I want to destroy something the same way he does. He could make another. Hell, I'll get him the fucking paper from the donation lounge at school.

Walking out, I almost drop my bag when I run into a brick wall. I look up to find two penetrating eyes rooting me to the spot.

Rey.

He doesn't approve of me being here. I don't know what I did to him, but I'll stay out of his way.

"I'm sorry," I say softly and move to leave, but he blocks me.

A stubborn tear escapes. I look up, and he walks me back to the office. The light automatically turns on.

"I need to get going," I tell him. "It's late."

It's late, I need to find a safe place to park. Food is out of the question.

I follow his gaze to the torn origami, the money, and the sweatbands I left in his bin. Not caring about what he thinks, I turn to go, but he grabs my hand, and slowly, before I have time to snatch my hand from his grasp, he wipes my tear with his thumb. I'm frozen under his touch.

He shakes his head slowly, but I try to tell him silently with my eyes that I want things to be different. I want us to get along.

He tries to hand me the money. He motions for me to sit at the desk when I don't take it. I let out a sigh in defeat and take a seat.

He folds the bill into different sections as quickly as he can. After a minute, he places an origami heart of the fifty-dollar bill near the keyboard on the desk. It is impressive, and I'm sure he doesn't think I would tear it up. He pulls out the gift and slides it over his wrists.

"You don't have to wear them if you don't want to," I rush out. "I wasn't sure if you would like them, and if you don't, I understand."

He nods when he turns to look at me with them on. I instinctively rub my finger over the material, it feels like a soft cotton towel. They're perfect on him.

His eyes lift, and I see something soft grow in them. There isn't a glimpse of anger, but someone with passion—a heart. I can see it. The way he is looking at me right now is how women beg to be looked at—like you're different, and words aren't good enough.

I get up, causing him to take two steps back. He towers over me. He must be about six foot three, maybe taller. His gym T-shirt stretches over his chest muscles. The width of his neck looks like two of my thighs combined. Intimidating, strong, and powerful. But God, he is gorgeous. When he looks at me like that, my heart races. My mind begs for him to say something. I want to understand him. I want to hear his voice so I could imagine what it would be like if he said my name.

Just one word.

Instead, his gaze falls to my lips. In a flash, and all the energy is sucked out of the room. I pull my hand away, careful my fingers don't graze his skin. Afraid he would retreat into his shell, worried that I wouldn't be able to stop myself.

"Thank you," I whisper.

The office grows quiet. I hear his steady breathing and smell his masculine scent. A shiver runs down my body. My stomach clenches under his gaze. I'm attracted to him. I wish I could swim in his eyes forever, but I can't.

He's a fighter, and I'm a survivor.

My reality awaits me outside these walls, where it is cold and unforgiving.

We are two different people from different worlds, but no one has made me feel the way he does.

REV

THE LAST PERSON leaves the gym. I walk to the punching bag in the rear, which gives me a good view of the front door. I usually lock it so I don't worry about someone walking inside. But Aria hasn't left.

I'm unsure what's keeping her from leaving, and I'm not going to find out. If I spend a minute alone with her in a room with no one around, I couldn't stop myself. The last time I was alone with her, I saw how upset she was when I ignored her when she went to hand me the gift. It was like something was dying inside me. The look of sadness that crossed her beautiful face broke me.

I was conflicted.

A part of me wanted to tell her the truth, and the other part wanted her to hate me so I had a reason to stay away from her. Not make her a little origami swan like a lovesick fool. I wasn't thinking when I left it for her. I had fallen asleep in the office and then woke up thinking of her. The way swans do when they find their fated mate.

I had to make it right that night. I couldn't let her pay me back for buying her lunch. She looked thin. Tired. It wasn't my business, but I couldn't let her go home thinking I didn't want any part of her because I did. I didn't want anyone to have the image of her in their eyes. That part of her while she was still here was mine.

I hated when guys gave her hungry looks. The way Mike did when he was fucking her with his eyes when she walked in that day. Anger fired up my blood, and I took the opportunity to show him. So when he looked at himself in the mirror, he remembered who did it.

Ari was innocent in that way. The way a woman is when she doesn't know how dirty a man's mind can be when he wants something he isn't supposed to have.

She is vulnerable. You can smell it a mile away.

The light from the office bounces off the mirrors when the door opens. I hold the bag to keep it from moving and quickly move behind the pillar, waiting for her to leave so I can shower, lock up, and head home. I reach into my pocket for my phone and notice it's already half past eleven.

I wonder why she stayed so late. Maybe she got caught up with something Javier told her to do, or she had a test. I caught her studying during her break. Her work ethic is flawless, and I don't mind. I know she is smart and dedicated. Her timing is impeccable. It was the fact that I couldn't stop thinking about her since she walked through the front door.

She walks out of the office, shuts the light off, looks up, smiles, and waves. I turn around and grab my stuff, ignoring her like I always do when she tries to engage in conversation with me. I should stay away from her, but I couldn't keep my eyes off her. It was worse when she looked away disappointed because I didn't reply or acknowledge her. The light that would dim in her delicate features. My chest grew tight, and the anger would burn like a black flame.

All I wanted was to destroy. To scream in the silence of the noise.

I pick up the gym towel and car keys, glance at my phone with my headphones still on, act like I'm distracted by something on the screen, and wait with my back turned until she leaves.

ARI

I WAITED for what seemed like forever for everyone to leave. When I saw Rey, I waved like a stupid idiot. I've gotten used to his moods. One minute, he burns me up, and the next, he douses the flame, turning me to ashes. I was relieved when I saw he was done and picked up his keys.

I slammed the exit door and ran toward the locker room before he could see me when he turned around. I hide behind the tiled wall by the entrance of the locker room, so the sensors from the lights wouldn't go off. When I asked Javier to use the bathroom, he checked to see if anyone was inside the locker room. I didn't know they had showers. Like an idiot, I spent the last week trying to find a place to shower, but I came up empty. This was my only shot until I could save enough for an apartment.

When I hear the echo of the front door lock, I rush to an empty corner locker where I stuffed a small bag. The showers have dividers for some privacy. They do not have doors, but they are better than the shelter.

The lights shut off if it doesn't sense movement in a specific area. I choose the last stall, and the entrance lights shut off after three minutes.

I take a deep breath, place my bag on the hook, and turn on the shower. After I remove my clothes, I step into the spray. The warm water feels like heaven. For the first time in almost two weeks, I shaved every part of my body I couldn't in a public bathroom. The most I could do was my armpits.

Funny how you take things for granted. Who knows if I can do this tomorrow without getting caught. The water is hot, and I close my eyes and smile for the first time in a couple of days. Not the fake smile I give everyone to hide my desperation. The worst part of being alone is knowing everyone is watching you. Waiting for the cracks to show to take advantage.

Sometimes people take the little things for granted. A hot shower, a bed, a heater, and air-conditioning. I stick my tongue out, feeling the warm water. The scent of soap on my clean skin. There are nights when it feels like I've been stranded on an island without water to bathe. Cold that seeps deep in my bones in need of warmth.

I wash, shave, and try not to think about getting caught, but then, a sob breaks free from my chest. The wall I've been trying to keep holding up so no one can see how alone I feel crumbles. How much I want to crawl up and lay on a bed and go to sleep without worrying that someone might break my car window and attack me.

After five minutes, I blow my nose and wash my face again, not wanting to push my luck in case someone comes back.

I take the razor and shift my leg to shave the back of my knees. Getting to that spot is a pain, so I usually leave it for last. I'm finishing my second knee when I hear a noise and freeze.

Footsteps.

My hands begin to shake. My heart is beating so hard in my chest. My pulse hammers in my ears.

Oh my God. Shit!

Someone is in here. Rey was the last person to leave, and I didn't see anyone else with him. *You didn't check, Aria.* I was so focused on Rey, who is always the last person to leave the gym, that I didn't think there was someone else.

I shut the water off. I move slowly and reach to grab the

towel I left on the outer hook, but I can't get it without step-ping out of the stall.

Another shower turns on, the spray hammering against the tiles. Fear runs down my spine. Oh my God.

I try to remain still so the light above me will turn off, but it doesn't.

I remember the razor in my hand, but it slips from my fingers and falls to the floor.

In one swift move, I snatch the towel off the hook and freeze.

Rey stands about three stalls down with his eyes open wide. I. Want. To. Just. Die. I move one arm over my chest in a lame attempt to cover my breasts, my other hand over my private parts, pushing my legs together, but it's stupid because the towel falls on the wet floor. Dammit.

Now, I'm trying to cover myself with my hands while Rey watches me completely naked. My lungs feel like they are starved of oxygen. He is big... everywhere.

He arches a brow. I'm embarrassed that I was caught star-ing. He turns, giving me a side view of his perfect ass. I bend my knees slowly, push my thighs together, and pick up the towel. It's heavy, drenched from the shower water, creating a puddle at my feet and most likely covered in germs.

My only option is to get a shirt from my bag to dry off.

When he turns back around, my eyes fall on his massive cock between his thighs.

When he moves, I screech, "What are you doing!"

I step back and almost slip when he moves to the side, opens a metal door, and reaches inside a silver box resembling a mini fridge. I don't wait to see what he is trying to get or do and open the towel wide like a screen to block his view of my naked body.

"I'm waiting for you to leave," I tremble. "You're freaking

me out!" I say, raising my voice, but he ignores me. "Why don't you answer me!"

Nothing.

I tear my gaze and measure the distance between where I am and the exit to the locker room, where my bag sits with my clothes and car key. I would have to make a run for it around him. It doesn't help that I'm naked. I quickly weigh my options. If I run, I could slip and fall. I don't stand a chance. He can knock me out with a flick of his finger and no effort. He can do anything he wants right now, but there isn't much I can do to stop it.

He doesn't seem like the type, but I wouldn't know. A series of shivers runs over my skin from the cold.

A tap on my left hand pulls me away from my thoughts. "What?"

He pushes a folded towel toward me and looks away. I sigh in relief and grab the soft white towel. Thank God. I wrap it around my naked body as fast as I can.

He gives me his back. My eyes drop to his muscular ass as he grabs another towel and wraps it around his waist. I stare at the tattoos on his skin. Skulls, angels, and a pair of gloves with flowers.

He turns around.

"Thank you. I appreciate you giving me a fresh towel." He blinks. I swallow, trying not to stare at his naked chest, and continue, "I'm sorry for being in here. I—"

He runs his fingers through his hair, causing his biceps to flex. My eyes trail over different shades of ink.

When my eyes reach his face, his jaw is set, his expression blank, and I just want the ground to open and swallow me whole.

He points at the exit, but I shake my head. "I'll get dressed, and I'll leave after you. I-I'm sorry for yelling, but..."

There is nothing I can say. I'm not supposed to be in here.

He points again, but I shake my head. Annoyed, he rolls his eyes.

I'm fired. I know I am.

He walks toward the locker room and removes his towel, drying himself while his ass muscles flex before he disappears around the corner.

I wait a minute before walking out to get dressed. He's probably waiting for me in the office to fire me, but he isn't. He's standing by my bag on the bench, dressed in sweatpants and a hoodie with his arms crossed over his chest.

I blink back my tears when reality sets in, but I can't help it. They fall down my cheeks. I'm back to square one. I have to find another job.

He straightens. My pride has me looking away. I should scream for him to get out, but I don't. I'm tired. He did the honorable thing and gave me a towel to cover up. He could call the police and say I trespassed after hours. He has every right to be here, and I don't.

When he steps closer, I stiffen and lower my head in defeat. His thumb slowly wipes the tears sliding down my cheeks, causing small tingles in his wake. He lifts my chin with an index finger, and my eyes slowly meet his in a silent plea. *Please don't fire me.* I know it's futile to voice it. He won't respond to anything I say. Hell, he tries to avoid me as much as possible. I tried too hard not to mess this up. To work hard. Not to arrive late and leave later than expected. I want to go above and beyond what I was hired to do, but it's too late. I crossed a line. A line you can't come back from. Similar to a thief. Not to be trusted.

I grab my stuff, walk to a bathroom stall, quickly get dressed, and walk out. I'm not surprised he is waiting for me to escort me out like I was shoplifting.

He points toward me and then to the door. I grip the strap on my bag, knowing what comes next, and follow him out.

———

He walks into the office. The light turns on, and he moves behind the desk and sits.

He avoids my gaze and scans the office. Everything is organized and labeled, clean and dusted before I left. The shirts that were in boxes on the floor are neatly folded and placed by size on a black shelf.

I sit in front of the desk and sag my shoulders in defeat.

There is no room for my pride right now.

You can do this, Ari. Let him fire you and leave gracefully. He didn't make a pass at me. He didn't act like a creep. I'm sure he has seen countless women naked, and I'm nothing special.

He was gentle and respectful.

I was confused when he placed his thumb on my cheek, wiping my tears away, but I knew it was because he felt sorry for what he had to do.

He leans forward and slides a paper from the notepad near the keyboard toward me. "Here's my phone number."

My eyebrows pinch in confusion. "You want me to call you?" I ask.

He rolls his eyes, slides the paper back, grabs a pen, writes something else below it, and slides it back again.

Is this a joke? Why can't he just tell me what he wants to say?

"Text me," I read aloud. He nods, waving his phone.

I lean back, slide my phone out of my bag, and enter his number as a thought enters my head. He wants to have it documented by text that I was trespassing after hours and found using the facilities without permission. It's the only thing that would make sense. There are no witnesses, and it could be hearsay.

There are cameras in the office and the main gym, but not in the locker rooms, for obvious reasons.

This is it. I should be as professional as I can under the circumstances. I'm not going to tell him why I needed to trespass and take a shower. I'm past humiliating myself further.

> Ari: Mr. Vicente,
>
> Thank you for the opportunity, and I'm sorry.
>
> Ari

He looks at the screen, waiting for my text to come through. I don't wait for him to read it and walk out.

What is the point? I'm fired.

I have to find a safe spot to park for the night. It's too late to get something to eat. The shelter isn't an option. The gas station locks up the main doors. The twenty-four-hour diner is too expensive for me right now. I adjust the beanie over my damp hair, bracing myself for the cold air.

I pop the trunk, open my suitcase, and grab three sweaters because I can't even afford a blanket. A decent one costs thirty dollars, and the dollar store doesn't carry them. I zip my suitcase and feel my phone ding with an incoming text.

> Rey: There is nothing to apologize for. I didn't know you would be in there, and I'm sorry if I frightened you. Where are you headed? I'll follow you to make sure you get home safe. Please call me Rey.

I sit in the car and stare at the text in disbelief. I read the text twice to ensure the cold didn't mess with my eyes.

He isn't firing me.

I look through the rearview mirror to see Rey walk over to a black Range Rover with black letters spaced out on the hood that read K I N G, where I think Rover should go.

> Ari: You're not firing me?

> > Rey: Why would I fire you? You had the entire office cleaned on the first day. No, I'm not firing you.

> Ari: But I snuck into the locker room to shower without permission.

> > Rey: I don't see the problem. I mean, yeah, it's kind of weird for a woman to want to use the shower in a men's boxing gym, but I'm not judging.

The light from the phone lights up his face, and I see his mouth form a grin.

Another text comes through.

> > Rey: Why do you stare at me like that?

He looks up and sees me watching through my rearview mirror because I don't have my windows tinted. I think about his question for a second. It's hard not to stare at him. He is a mystery—a gorgeous mystery. When he walks into a room, you feel the power emanating from him, and he doesn't have to say a word to anyone.

But I play it off.

Ari: Why don't you talk to me? And for the
record, I don't stare at you. You don't look
at me, so how would you know if I stare
at you?

He tilts his head back and laughs as he reads the text.

Rey: What does it look like we're doing?
I'm talking to you right now.

Ari: Is this your way of testing me?

He laughs again, and I notice that he texts fast. His fingers
fly over the keyboard of his smartphone.

Rey: Trust me, I've never had to test a
woman.

Ari: Cocky much?

I regret the text as soon as I hit send.

Rey: Hey, you asked. So will you tell me
where you're staying so I can follow you
home, or will we be here for the rest of the
night?

Shit. He can't know that I'm homeless and that I live in my
car. I look up and see that he's waiting.

Ari: That's ok. You don't have to do that. I
appreciate the offer, but I'm sure you have
to be up early.

Rey: It's no trouble. I'll feel better knowing
you got home safe. Javier said you're
staying on campus.

I hate to turn down his offer and seem unappreciative, but

I don't know what to do. I hate myself for lying to Javier, but I can't tell anyone.

Ari: It's ok, Rey. Have a good night.

Before he could argue the point further and make me feel even worse than I already did for lying, I dropped the phone in the passenger seat and turned the car on, wincing at the horrible noise. I pull out and drive off.

After a few minutes, I sigh in relief when he doesn't follow me.

————

Not having the time to look for another spot to park, I pull into the park's deserted parking lot and park under the same ancient tree. I check the locks and look around. When I see no one around, I grab the sweaters and hold them up to the vent, blowing hot air.

After a few minutes of warming the sweater, I pull it on and remove the beanie to dry my hair. It's the only way to dry my hair until my paycheck hits my bank account, and I can buy a hair-dryer and car adapter. After getting it as dry as possible, I shut the car off. Pushing the seat back as far as it can go, I turn off the engine and curl into the driver's seat.

I check my phone. It has a full charge to last me through the night, and I set my alarm for class in the morning.

I charge my phone in class or during my break in the library and at work at the boxing gym. I have a car charger, but I would have to leave my car running all night. My car doesn't have the feature of charging your device without the car being on.

My phone vibrates with an incoming text, and I grab it

from the cup holder, hoping it isn't Jimmy. He texts me at night with the same requests. That we are not over. To go home. I was tempted to block him but didn't know what he was up to. I thought he would let it go after a while. His practice runs while I'm at school. I don't think he will want to risk being penalized for missing practice.

When I open the text, I'm surprised to see that it's Rey.

Rey: Ari?

The reminder of what happened earlier sinks into my mind. The fear of losing is the only good thing I have going for me besides school and my job. The embarrassment of him seeing me nude in the shower, followed by the fear of being alone with a man I don't know. The pity in his eyes.

Ari: Yes, Rey.

Rey: Are you home?

I close my eyes when the tears cast down my face after I press send. Hating myself for trying to keep up with a lie. For some reason, I hate lying to him.

Ari: Yes. I made it. Thank you for asking, Rey.

It was nice of him to care if I got home safely. It could have been worse. At least he let me keep my job.

My phone pings again. I open my eyes, and a tear drops on the screen. I wipe the screen with my thumb.

Rey: Ari?

Ari: Yes, Rey.

> Rey: Can you turn around and unlock the
> door?

My stomach drops. I shift in my seat, stunned to see him standing outside the driver's side window.

He followed me.

I have no excuse to give him for why I'm parked and sleeping in my car right now. I can't push him away because I need the job working at the gym. If he wanted to hurt me, he would have.

I unlock the door with nervous fingers. He pulls the handle. The door widens, but I look away, not wanting him to see me cry. I see him hold his hand out from the corner of my eyes.

I look over my shoulder. I can't see his face clearly from the tears in my eyes, but I take his outstretched hand. It's strong and firm when he pulls me gently out of the car. I cross my arms over my chest tight like I'm wearing a straitjacket when the cold wind hits my warm skin.

"What are you doing here?" I ask.

After a few seconds, he still doesn't respond. I look up, and our eyes meet. He gestures for me to step aside but doesn't wait for me to move. He manages to slide inside the car with his big body and hands me my phone, backpack, sweater that fell to the floorboard, and charger. He then takes my keys out of the ignition. He glances in the back seat, gets out, shuts the door, and locks it.

"What are you doing?" I ask again, but as always, he doesn't answer. He uses my key to open my trunk and grabs my suitcase. I move in front of him. "What are you doing with my suitcase?"

He ignores me, grabs my hand, and pulls me gently across the parking lot to his Range Rover. He opens the passenger door and places my suitcase in the back. Not wanting to fight him because I'm tired and cold, I slide into the most luxurious car I have ever been inside. It smells like expensive cologne with a hint of cedar.

He turns my chin to face him and does the same thing he did in the locker room. He wipes the wet tears off my cheek with his thumb. My eyes find his. Our gazes hold for a few seconds before he reaches over me and grabs the seat belt to buckle me in.

"Where are you taking me?"

He blinks. I sigh, lay my head back on the headrest, and watch him. He takes a deep breath, looks at his phone, and texts me.

My phone pings. I scrunch my brows in confusion. I pick up my phone and read.

> Rey: I don't understand what you are saying.

What does he mean? I'm right here.

I look up, but he's staring at his phone. Is this a joke? I text him.

> Ari: I'm talking to you. Do you understand what I'm saying?

> Rey: I'm deaf, Aria.

Deaf? What does he mean, deaf? I've seen him interact with Javier, and he wears headphones. How is he deaf?

I look up, and he waits. He can't be. How is that possible?

> Ari: What do you mean you're deaf?

> Rey: It means I can't hear what you are saying. I can pick up most things from your lips. I have progressive hearing loss.

I know what deaf means. That's not really what I'm asking, but...

> Ari: Why didn't you tell me?

I've been talking to him like an idiot, and the whole time, he couldn't hear me.

> Rey: It's not like I go around with a sign that says I'm deaf. I can read your lips. I'm pretty good at it since I used to be able to hear.

I feel like a total ass. I've judged him this whole time for not introducing himself when he walked into the office. Guilt claws at my chest. How could I have missed it? I feel like such an ass.

> Ari: Do you know what I just said?

> Rey: All I picked up on was, "Where are you taking me?"

I look over at him, and he gives me a half shrug.

> Ari: I'm sorry. I'm embarrassed about everything that has happened tonight.

He gives me a sympathetic expression, nods, and then types back.

> Rey: Don't be. You had a valid reason.

He smiles. I admire his full lips and strong hands as they hold the phone, and his thumbs fly across the keyboard.

> Rey: Are you in this situation because of your ex-boyfriend?

My brows pinch. How does he know about Jimmy? Of course... Javier.

> Ari: Javier told you.

He nods.

> Rey: He did. I'm sorry, but I can't let you sleep in your car. It's not safe. You can stay with me and Javier. I have a spare room you can use until you get on your feet. I won't charge you rent or anything.

I shake my head. No way can I stay in a house with two professional fighters. Not to mention that both are my bosses.

> Ari: I appreciate it, Rey, but I can't work for you and not pay rent. It feels like I'm taking advantage of you and Javier.

> Rey: Ari, I'm not going to leave you here. I can't. It's no trouble. I have plenty of spare bedrooms. It would be nice to have company. Javier will be mad if I don't insist you stay with us.

I have two options: I can stay alone in the parking lot and freeze to death once the temperature drops, or I can take his offer until I find an apartment.

I glance at him after I hit send.

Ari: Okay. Only until I have saved enough to find my own place. It shouldn't take long. Are you sure Javier will be okay with me staying at your house? Will your girlfriend or Javier be upset?

He smiles and then laughs. Flutters swirl in my stomach. It's a nice laugh. Deep and genuine.

Rey: We've never had a female besides our mother live with us. After I won my first fight, I bought myself a place. Javier decided to live with me and I bought a nice home for my mom. We have lived together ever since. My mother lives an hour away, next door to my aunt.

I'm not sure if I should feel nervous or relieved.

REY

I PLACE my phone in the cupholder, relieved she's agreed to stay with us. I was shocked to find her in the shower.

After seeing her naked, all I could think about was the curve of her breasts and the indent of her waist down to her freshly shaved pussy. She is even more beautiful without her clothes on. I couldn't look away but forced myself to do the noble thing and get her a towel.

There has to be a reason she snuck into the locker room to take a shower. Many things don't make sense about Ari, things she is hiding, and things I intend to discover.

Javier didn't tell her I was deaf because I asked him not to. I wanted it to be up to me to tell her. I wanted it to be my choice. We have an agreement that I get to choose who I tell. I needed to tell her at some point, but I was afraid of her reaction. I didn't want to see pity in her eyes, but finding her sleeping in her car brought forth a protective instinct inside me that I could never ignore when it came to her.

We all have secrets we want to keep from people because we're afraid they will see we are different, that we lack something we need, or that we have a weakness.

After driving for five minutes, I find an all-night diner. The moon is nowhere to be found in the dark sky. It's late, but I didn't see her eat while she was at the gym. When I followed her to ensure she got home safely, I parked on the side of the road, not believing what I saw. She has nowhere to go. Javier has mentioned an ex-boyfriend, but what kind of monster would put her in this situation? There has to be a reason. I couldn't sleep at night knowing I left her alone, sleeping in her car in a deserted park. What if something happened and I wasn't there to stop it? I wouldn't be able to forgive myself.

My eyes swing to her, and I watch her type on her phone. The light from her screen shines across her face.

Ari: Why are we here?

Rey: Are you hungry? I noticed you didn't eat anything since you came into the gym.

Ari: It's ok, Rey. You have done enough by offering me a place to stay.

Rey: Ari, don't fight me about this. Please, I want to.

My eyes plead with hers. Seconds feel like years as I watch her lips. I could watch her all night. I didn't realize I was holding my breath when she nodded and removed her seat belt.

ARI

ONCE REY and I are seated, the server places the menus in front of us. I watch him as he scans the menu while I try to process the fact that he is deaf.

> Ari: I hope you don't mind me asking. How do you communicate with strangers when you're out? I'm not sure if I should order for you or if that would offend you. To be honest, I have never been around someone who is deaf.

He places his forearms on the table with his phone in hand. I follow the lines of his straight nose, which has a slight imperfection on the bridge, probably from being broken. His dark hair, tan skin, and tattoos are visible on the tops of his hands. When he trains, his hands are usually wrapped with athletic tape or he wears boxing gloves.

When he stops, I tear my gaze away reluctantly and wait for the notification from my phone.

> Rey: My usual method is to point at the menu, jot it down on paper, or type it on my phone to show the server. It's straightforward. No one really questions it. They understand my needs, and I settle the bill. It's as easy as that. Just so you know, your questions aren't offensive to me.

When I finish reading the text, the server appears, and I ask for water. She looks at Rey, waiting for him to order. My phone goes off.

> Rey: I would like water and the number three with no bread.

I tell the server our order.

> Ari: You understood when I asked for water?

He looks at me and smiles. I swear my heart skipped a beat.

> Rey: I can read your lips.

> Ari: Everyone's or just certain people?

> Rey: Not everyone, but I can read yours.

> Ari: How come?

> Rey: They are easy to follow.

He looks up from his phone. His eyes fall to my lips, mine to his. His lips are full. Two old scars in the form of white lines on the left side of his mouth make him appear more rugged. Real. His scars are imperfections that I find attractive.

When our food arrives, I notice he waits until he sees me take a bite of my club sandwich before he starts eating. I can't help but wonder how he manages to train his brother in the gym, being deaf. How does he communicate in the boxing ring? It's fascinating how people don't know. How no one has realized he can't hear them. I also can't help but notice the headphones he wears.

When I looked him up online, there was no mention of Rey being deaf, no tabloid or TMZ article. It only mentioned his achievements as a fighter. He is the number one pound-for-pound fighter in the world right now. The latest news is that the undefeated heavyweight fighter of the world is training his brother for his upcoming debut.

———

After a fifteen-minute drive, he turns onto a single road. It's dark, and only the headlights of his car allow me to see. He stops in front of a metal gate and presses the garage door button from his car. The automatic gates swing open.

The car crawls down the paved driveway until his house comes into view. The huge house is impressive, with a circular driveway and a seven-car garage. The landscape is professionally done, with topiaries surrounding the pavers. Two large windows have modern drapes on each side of the black double doors and two fall wreaths. The elegant house is contemporary in design.

He presses another button from his car, and one of the garage doors opens automatically.

The garage floors gleam against the white garage lights as he pulls in. He gets out and walks over to the back of his car, where he removes my suitcase. When he closes the back door, I receive a text.

> Rey: Welcome to my home. Javier is asleep and will be up soon for his morning run. He knows we made it home. I hope that's alright. I had your car towed to the gym from the park. Follow me so I can show you to the guest bedroom.

> Ari: Thank you, Rey. Thank you for allowing me to stay in your gorgeous home.

> Rey: My pleasure.

I want to dissolve in a puddle. There are no words to express how grateful I am for his hospitality. I regret the way I spoke to him in the locker room.

Tears well up in my eyes as I realize I get to sleep in a bed. It feels like ages since I felt a soft pillow, stretched my legs, did not have a seat belt buckle into my side, or woke up feeling cold.

As I follow him inside, we pass the living room with bone-colored marble flooring and black accented furniture. The furniture is minimal, and the walls have thin-lined sconces with sensor lighting.

He stops when we reach the grand staircase and gestures for me to follow him.

I watch his muscles bunch and flex as he ascends the stairs with my suitcase in his right arm as if it weighs nothing.

He stops before a door and opens it with his free hand to a beautiful, decorated room with dark wood furniture and the same bone-colored marble tile. The queen-sized bed is already turned down. The lamp glows across the room, giving off a luxurious feel like I'm staying at a five-star hotel.

He sets my suitcase down in front of the bed. He looks up as soon as he sends me a text.

> Rey: I hope you like the room. The bathroom is right through the door to the left. Have a good night, Aria. I'll see you in the morning.

> Ari: Thank you, Rey. The room is perfect. Good night. Please call me Ari.

My mouth curves into a grin, and I surprise him by standing on my toes and kissing his cheek softly.

He leans his head slightly. It feels like the sun's heat is on my skin, warming me up inside. Like a light has been turned on after so many days of darkness. I don't want to pull away. I want him to hold me, but I know that's impossible. He's my boss, and I cannot feel anything but professionalism and gratitude for what he has done for me tonight. He pulls away and exits the room, taking the heat and light with him.

I unzip my suitcase to change into a pair of pajamas. I slide under the soft sheets and hide under the blankets as needles prick my throat, and the tears come.

REY

I ALMOST STAYED in instead of going with Javier for a six-mile run. All I can think about is Ari in my guest bedroom. Her lips are as soft as they look.

I wanted to drag her to my bedroom and keep her warm. I told her she was safe with me. There was more that I wanted to do than hold her. So I took a cold shower.

Smoke swirls in the air with each breath I take. Javier matches my pace. He won't last in the ring if he can't keep up.

We pass the midway point and are soon at the end of the trail. The cool, thin air burns my lungs as I take deep breaths. It feels like my lungs are on fire. I'm pushing myself. The cold freezes my skin from my sweat. I want to go back home and see if she is up. If she slept comfortably enough. Who knows how long she has been sleeping in her car.

Javier stops. He places his palms on his bent knees, out of breath. It looks like he's cooking barbecue from all the smoke from his nose and mouth.

"I can't believe you followed her, and she was sleeping in her car," Javier says, shaking his head between breaths.

I nod, telling him I understood what he said. I didn't tell him about the shower incident because he would give me shit about it. Plus, I don't feel comfortable discussing Aria. She looked defeated. Broken.

In the gym, she always looks cheerful and bright. Waving

when she sees me. A pretense to what she is going through. A way to hide the truth. She's homeless. It makes me feel like shit for ignoring her when I first met her.

Javier opens the front door. I slide my damp hoodie over my head and freeze. If I weren't deaf, I would hear my stomach growl in protest. The most delicious smell of French toast causes my stomach to scream.

"Oh my God. It smells like heaven in here," Javier signs to me with a smile.

When we get closer to the kitchen, Ari is bent over, reaching into the refrigerator, wearing the shortest pajama shorts I have ever seen. She hasn't noticed us.

Javier angles his head to the side, admiring the view. He turns to look at me with a smile on his face. He makes a motion with his hands in a mocking gesture about her ass while biting his bottom lip.

Her ass is very nice, more than nice, but I try not to look at her perfect ass cheeks that peek out the bottom of her shorts.

Javier keeps his eyes trained on her ass. I slap him upside the head.

"What?" he signs.

I shake my head and sign back, "She works for us. Stop it."

"Come on, Rey. I know that, but you cannot deny that I made the right choice." He smiles. "Ari is hot. I think we need to just let her live here permanently. Maybe she will just walk around dressed like that all day."

I slap him playfully upside the head again. This is what happens when you're training for a fight. No woman. No sex. It has him stupid.

He rubs the side of his head with a laugh, which gets Ari's attention. I watch her lips move as she says, "*Hi*," but her eyes are glued to mine.

Javier gives her a big smile, then removes his hoodie so we

are both bare-chested. Asshole. I didn't do it to show off. It was so I wouldn't get sick. He doesn't seem to care that she works for us.

I smile and then turn to Javier. "Stop showing off," I sign.

He rolls his eyes. "Stop being a grouch. You were checking out her ass, too. I saw you. Don't act like you don't think she is hot. You keep riding me about her. I think she is fine. The guys in the gym think she is fine."

My nostrils flare. "Make sure you tell all the guys in the gym that Ari is a no-fly zone. That goes for you, too. No chatting her up while training or flirting in the gym. We train fighters to be champions, not set them up on dates."

"Fine. I'll let her know that she can't flirt with the guys in the gym, and she isn't there to pick up guys. Got it."

When I look at Ari, her smile is replaced by a disappointed look. I realize what Javier signed, he also spoke out loud.

She says something to Javier, but I'm focused on how I want to punch Javier for telling her what I said so I don't catch it.

He turns to me and signs, "She said for you not to worry about her trying to pick up guys at the gym. She isn't interested in being involved with anyone. Especially athletes. In her experience, they don't know how to treat women."

"Tell her thank you for understanding. I'm sorry her experience with athletes didn't work out for her, but we cannot afford distractions at the gym," I sign as Javier speaks, relaying the message.

She ignores me and begins to plate our breakfast, placing it on the table. Each plate has fluffy scrambled eggs, French toast with butter and syrup, napkins, and utensils. Javier glares at me, not caring that he is breaking his meal plan as he sits down and begins to eat.

I feel like shit for saying what I said. It is none of my business. I shouldn't care who she talks to, but I do. I hate the way I made her feel. I hate that she doesn't look at me like I want her to. I hate that I took away her smile, but what I hate the most is that I can't tell her I'm sorry.

ARI

JAVIER WAS nice enough to take me to the gym that morning to pick up my car. I was glad it wasn't Rey. For the past three weeks, I have stayed away from Rey as much as possible. What he said to me that day in the kitchen stung. What he thought of me made me realize he gave me a place to stay out of pity. He needed someone to work at the gym and was being a good human by not letting me sleep in my car.

I understand he is setting boundaries and laying down rules as his employee, but it hurts that he thinks so little of me. What did I expect? He caught me using the shower without permission and found me sleeping in my car after I lied to him.

I'm grateful he gave me a place to stay, but what he said was a slap to my face. It felt like a bucket of cold water dumped over my head. I would have walked out if it wasn't for the fact that I had nowhere to go.

The best way to deal with it all was to avoid looking at him. I avoid him whenever I can. If I need to speak to him, I text him or use Javier. I'm determined to pinch every penny.

Since that first morning, I haven't eaten out or cooked in their house. I stick to gas station food and one- dollar drinks. I eat ramen noodles and heat them on campus before I get to work.

The less money I spend, the sooner I can move into my own place.

I thought about learning ASL. I hated not being able to communicate. I'm sure others less fortunate than Rey need a job.

So when I needed an elective for my last semester, I saw that ASL was available and signed up for it. I made a goal to learn twenty to thirty words a week in addition to what the course requires. I also watch YouTube videos.

I have been going in and out of the office supply room behind the punching bags to the left side of the gym. From the corner of my eye, I can see Rey in the ring demonstrating to the guys how to use a rope with his chin tucked near his shoulder and weaving in and out.

There are times I keep hidden so I can watch him teach. I admire his passion in the ring and the way he cares. You can see the awe in the other members' eyes when he steps into the ring. It is fascinating that he doesn't have to say a word, and they all watch and listen. I admire the respect he gets.

I'm in the office reviewing the sign-up forms attached to the waivers, ensuring all forms are filled out and the waivers signed. Two guys attend Penn State, and I'm glad I don't recognize the names. I'm trying to avoid anyone who knows Jimmy. Jimmy continues to send me random text messages that I ignore. I hope he will leave me alone with time and accept that nothing he says or does will get me to go back.

I look up when Javier walks into the office. "Hey," he greets me with a smile.

"Hey. Did you need something?"

He takes a seat. "Are you okay?"

"Yep."

I haven't been upbeat or wanting to start conversations. I'm hardly at their house unless it's to shower or sleep. I try to stay out of their way. I left my bedroom the same way I found it and kept my clothes inside my suitcase in case.

"Are you sure?"

I nod and try to give him my best fake smile. "Of course."

He lowers his voice. "I don't mean to be nosy, but some-times I hear you cry at night."

My cheeks flame from embarrassment. I didn't think he could hear me.

I slide a strand of my hair behind my ear. "I'm sorry," I say. "I'm... getting over it."

He thinks I mean Jimmy, but it's the situation I'm trying to get over.

"I think you're doing a great job." He waves his hands around the office. "The office looks great. I'm unsure if Rey has told you how impressed we are."

"He hasn't, but thank you."

He pinches his eyebrows, and his jaw hardens. "He hasn't told you that? Sent a message?"

I shake my head. "No. But that's okay. I don't expect anything. You both have done a lot for me. I see that you're working hard. Your dedication and drive to want to be the best. I know you're going to win."

He smiles. "You think so, huh."

I give him a genuine smile in return. "I know it. I kinda sneaked a peek at the other guy's last fight on YouTube."

"Are you spying for me?" he teases.

I rub my lips together, trying to stifle a laugh. "Of course, I have to make sure my boss wins. I have to see what he doesn't see."

"I knew I made the right choice offering you the job." He gives me a smirk. "I don't regret it," he says before he walks out.

Looking out the office window, I notice a pair of brown eyes looking at me from the boxing ring. I quickly avert my gaze. Not everyone has the same opinion.

Around five o'clock, I see the two members who need to

sign waivers walk inside the gym. When I read their profiles, they both have amateur fight cards but didn't sign their waivers when they signed up to train here.

It is my job to make sure everything is completed and filed. They can't train because it would be a liability if something happened and they got hurt.

I'm working on entering payments into the ledger for the week, so I wait to catch them when they walk from the locker room.

When they finally step out, they head to the boxing ring, where Rey and Javier work on technique. Rey has his headphones on, as always, and motions to Javier with his hands between punches. It takes a lot of effort, and I try not to look at him or the way his muscles flex with each punch.

They don't see me when I approach. I reach the side of the ring where the guys are watching and tap the first one named Tommy.

He turns around. His eyes scroll over me suggestively, and it makes me want to gag.

"Um... I'm sorry to bother you. Your name is Tommy, correct?"

He looks down at the clipboard and quirks a brow. "Yeah, I'm Tommy."

"I need you to sign this waiver right now, please. If not, you can't train."

"I'll sign it after I'm done training."

He turns around, giving me his back. What a dick. I take a deep breath and tap him on the shoulder again.

He turns around and licks his lips. He claps both of his hands like he is praying and says sarcastically, "Listen, you are hella fine and all, but I can't talk right now. Maybe when I'm done. I can take you out and do whatever it is you want me to do for you."

I roll my eyes, wanting to punch him. A guy with brown hair and a Penn State T-shirt walks up, his brows raised in recognition when his gaze lands on me.

He runs his fingers through his damp hair. "Yo, Tommy. Chill, man."

Tommy looks over. "What, Ben? She wants me to sign some, and I don't feel like signing shit right now." He waves his hand to dismiss me. "Go back to the office and look pretty. I promise to swing by later."

My skin flushes in anger. I have had just about enough of this asshole. I slap the back of the clipboard to his chest. His eyes widen. "I think you have the wrong idea. Sign it, or you don't train."

Tommy steps forward, causing me to step back. The clipboard falls on the mat between us. Tommy's top lip curls in a snarl. My stomach curls in knots. From the corner of my eye, I can see Javier removing the Velcro and nudging Rey, getting his attention.

Ben steps between Tommy and me. "Sign the waiver, man. She's just doing her job. Why do you have to be such a dick to her? Besides, do you know who she is?"

Tommy shakes his head. Who the fuck cares. Ben steps aside while another guy behind him tells Javier what happened. Rey's expression hardens, but when I think it's aimed at Tommy, it's directed at me. I'm confused because all I'm doing is my job and saving him from a potential lawsuit. Rey has it all wrong.

Rey angrily points his finger toward me and then points toward the office, telling me to go.

"Your name is Ari, right?" Ben asks. Shit. He knows.

Ben follows me when I bend down to pick up the clipboard. "Yeah," I say softly.

"You're Jimmy Harding's girlfriend." I shake my head. "Not anymore."

Ben hands me the pen from the floor when I straighten. "That's not what he says."

"Shit," Tommy mutters.

Looking at Ben, Javier asks, "Who's Jimmy?"

"Jimmy Harding, pro hockey player. Just got signed to the Flyers. Aria's his girlfriend. They live together."

"We broke up, and I moved out," I say but don't meet his eyes.

My eyes meet Rey's hard stare, which penetrates me like lasers. His jaw is clenched, and he looks angry. I'm not sure what he's thinking right now, but whatever it is, it's not good. Fear replaces the knots in my gut when he walks out of the ring. He walks up to me and stands like a brick wall blocking my view. I swallow the fear rising like bile in my throat. My knuckles grip the edge of the clipboard. Anger and disappointment swirl in his gaze.

I step back when his eyes harden. Javier shakes his head at Rey, but he doesn't care. Rey's nostrils flare. I flinch when he lifts his arm to point at the office. My pulse beats hard in my ears.

I bolt toward the office. Javier runs after me.

MY BOTTOM LIP QUIVERS. I scan the office for my bag and car keys. Javier's expression is full of worry when he follows me inside. I freeze when he steps closer.

"Javier," I say, breathless, like I was gut-punched. "I-I need to go right now. Please."

"I'm sorry, Ari. Please don't be scared. Rey... he would never hurt you. You know that, right? He's my brother, and I know he would never... I would never hurt you. You're safe with us."

I don't answer him and just point at the desk. I'm trying to calm down, but I can't stay here.

"I-I was just trying... to get Tommy to sign the waiver. He can't train until he does. There is another member who didn't sign. I-I was trying, but he was rude and..."

My eyes widen in panic when Rey walks in. I back away. "I want to leave," I demand in a shaky breath.

A pained look crosses Javier's face, and then he glances at Rey.

Rey looks tormented when he sees my bag over my shoulder and keys in my hand, but all I can think about is running.

He steps in front of Javier, but Javier puts a hand on his chest to stop him and shakes his head. Rey looks at Javier's hand on his chest and then at me.

Rey slides his phone out and begins typing. He looks up at me when my phone dings.

> Rey: Are you afraid of me?

When I nod, his fingers fly across his screen, and he looks up.

> Rey: I'm sorry. I didn't mean to frighten you. I was just upset about the interruption.

> Ari: I want to leave.

> Rey: Can we talk? Alone?

> Ari: I have nothing to say to you. I'll get my stuff and go. I don't want to be here.

Tears escape. Fear. Hurt. How defenseless I felt with him.

Before I know what is happening, Javier exits the room and shuts the door, leaving me alone with Rey.

> Rey: Please, let me prove that you shouldn't be scared of me. I'll never hurt you, Ari. Never.

He slides his phone into his pocket and tilts his head with a smile breaking his lips. He gives me a wink and motions for me to walk toward the door.

I move forward, and he steps behind me.

I turn around, and he cages me in, stealing my breath. My back is to the door, and his arms are on either side of my head. My chin quivers.

His eyes caress my face.

He reaches over and closes the blinds without breaking eye

contact. He lowers his lips near my ear; his breath tickles my skin, washing away my fear.

The grip on my bag relaxes.

I close my eyes, willing my fast heartbeat to calm. Everything goes quiet except for the faint voices outside.

Then... I hear it.

"I'm so sorry, Ari. Please don't leave me. I need you here," he says, just above a whisper.

The deep, raspy, and perfect sound of his voice. Soft like a caress over my skin.

My head tilts. His eyes hold me captive.

His lips graze the skin below my ear. "Don't move..."

His voice enraptures me as his hand wraps gently around my throat. His thumb is on the spot where my pulse beats.

His lips are inches from my skin, his breath feathering my cheek. His thumb slides back and forth, caressing my neck. His palm lays flat above me against the door.

His brown eyes turn to molten chocolate when they fixate on my lips. The power of his gaze draws me closer. Then... it happens.

His lips crash against mine, and I think I whimper when his tongue slides into my mouth.

I drop my bag with a thud. My keys with a clink. My hands land on his chest, sliding to his neck, feeling the hard- ness of his muscles. His tongue licks mine, the roof of my mouth, and then he sucks my lips.

We have to stop.

He is my boss, and I'm his employee.

A line has been crossed, but I don't want to go back over it yet.

I want to stay.

Just for another moment.

His hands dig in my hair. My chest is pressed against his,

and I want to hide in his warmth. Burn with the heat of his tongue.

I don't want it to be all over when he stops, which scares me the most. It scares me because I'm not afraid of him. It scares me because I want more.

He pulls away, and we're both out of breath. He feels it, but I hear it. What just happened wasn't supposed to happen, but it did, and it's boiling between us.

He rests his forehead on mine and whispers, "I'm sorry, but I'm not sorry. I know it shouldn't have happened, but I wanted it to happen. It can't happen again, and for that, I'm sorry. Please... Please don't leave, Ari. I would never hurt you." His voice breaks on the last part.

We are attracted to each other. He was frustrated and took it out on me, which I misinterpreted, thinking he would harm me.

I grip his gray shirt molded to his chest. My eyes find his. I reach for him on my tippy-toes. He knows what I want. His lips meet mine again, and I taste him thoroughly. I lick the seam of his lips and suck them. He groans in my mouth, gripping the side of my shirt in a fist. His lips skim my jaw, suck and bite my neck. My heart pounds. My nose fills with his scent. Sweat and cedar. My knees tremble, but he holds me to him, and I feel it was a promise. A promise not to let go.

When we break apart, he steps back and bends to pick up my bag and keys. He places them on the corner desk by the wall. He grabs the clipboard, looks at the two waivers, and slides his finger to the "X," where it is highlighted needing a signature.

He takes his phone and sends me a text.

> Rey: I'm sorry for not backing you up. You were just trying to do your job and looking out for our interest in the gym. I'm going to make it right.

> Ari: Don't scare me like that again.

> Rey: I promise, Ari. If there is an issue, you come to me. I don't want you to go to anyone in this gym without me.

My eyes lift.

> Ari: I'm sorry for not telling you. I don't want you to deal with gym-related paperwork while training Javier. This is important to him, and he needs you right now. He will win with you in his corner, but he needs every moment with you. Distractions cause mistakes. You needed someone here to work in the office while you trained Javier, and that was what I was trying to do. It's why Javier hired me.

He nods and moves to open the door. He waves his hand for me to step out first. Javier is in the ring, sparring with Tommy. Javier has a lethal glare painted on his face, and I'm surprised he's in the ring with Tommy.

Rey holds the clipboard, takes the waiver out, and motions for me to follow.

When Rey reaches the ring, he rings the bell. Javier pauses, but Tommy goes in for a punch. Javier sees just in time, blocks it, and then spits out his mouthpiece.

"What the fuck?" Javier spits.

Tommy waves his hands out wide and shrugs. This pisses Rey off. He rings the bell more forcefully and motions for Tommy to get out of the ring.

Tommy removes his mouthpiece. "What'd I do?" Tommy asks, glaring at me "What did you do, huh?" Tommy turns to Rey. "You fuckin' her, champ?"

Javier comes up behind him and pushes Tommy. "Watch what the fuck you say, Tommy. Apologize to Ari."

Tommy turns around and gets in Javier's face.

Having seen enough, Rey gets in the ring while crumpling the paper in his fist. I step back, my eyes going wide. Oh shit. The expression on Rey's face as he steps up to Tommy has everyone in the gym rushing over.

Tommy turns around and sees Rey.

He points his glove toward me. "Don't get mad, champ. It's all good. I know you're fucking her. She doesn't even look at any other guy in this place. Now everyone knows why she isn't with Jimmy. She's quick. I'll give her that," he taunts.

Fucking asshole. I have never wanted to punch somebody so badly in their smug face. I thought hockey players were dicks, but boxers are bigger dicks.

"Get out," Rey growls.

Oh my God. He spoke. Javier raises his eyebrows as he looks at Rey but remains quiet.

Tommy doesn't agree, so he shakes his head. "Nah, I'm not going to go because you have a hard-on for your office girl."

Rey curls his lip and gets in Tommy's face. Tommy rears his head back, laughing sarcastically. "I struck a nerve. You're always silent, but when I talk about her, you have no problem speaking," he sneers. "Wait until Jimmy finds out that Rey Vicente is FUCKING his girl."

"Get out, Tommy!" Javier shouts. "Don't come back to this gym or this camp. You're done."

"Fuck that. You're only fighting because your brother is the champ. I'll take both of you pussies out. I can't believe you're getting pissed off because I didn't want to sign a stupid paper when she wanted. She must be a nice piece of ass, Rey. What did she do, huh? Suck your dick in the office when you got mad at her for talking to me."

He pushes Rey, placing his gloved hands on his chest, but Rey is like a solid concrete wall. He doesn't budge. I'm grateful he can't hear the crap Tommy is spewing about me.

I can tell Javier is worried that Rey might lose his composure. The tension on Rey's face says it all. He wants to hit Tommy. I can feel it, and I think everyone else in the gym can feel it, too.

Tommy looks over at me, blows me a kiss, and makes a lewd gesture over his crotch. That's when it happens. Rey hits him with a left hook, knocking Tommy's headgear off his head, and he lands with a thud—knocked out.

"Oooh, shit!" one guy yells.

"Dayum!" another one calls.

"He deserved it. Tommy was way out of line," Ben says.

I look around and see a guy in shock, placing his hand over his head.

I look up at Rey. He isn't looking at Tommy or Javier. His chest heaves with pent-up rage, and he is looking directly at me.

I mouth, "I'm sorry."

He shakes his head and walks over to the ropes. He opens and closes his hand, probably feeling the impact of his fist connecting with Tommy's jaw.

Rey swallows, catching his breath. "I'll never let"—he takes a deep breath—"anyone... disrespect you, Ari."

His voice is louder than it should be. A little off pitch.

He battles his emotions, and I can't control mine. I'm powerless when he looks at me and cling desperately to the memory of being in his arms.

REY

JAVIER AND BEN ESCORT TOMMY out of the gym, and I immediately text my lawyer. He assures me everything will be fine. Tommy didn't want to leave and was combative because he didn't want to sign the waiver. Nothing he can do will jeopardize me or the gym.

When it comes to Ari, I lose control. When she's nearby, all I can think about is her smile and the way she looks at me when she thinks I don't notice. I notice everything about her, but I'll do anything to show her that I'll never physically harm her. I'll never let her think she has a reason to fear me.

When Tommy talked to her, I could only pick up a few words and piece them together. I was frustrated. I couldn't hear. I couldn't protect her when she needed me. When she said she was afraid of me, I could only show her why she shouldn't. A part of me died inside when she wanted to leave. My silence broke. It broke...for her.

Javier told me how she cries at night. He heard her one night when he passed by her room. I wanted to go in and hold her, but I knew she wasn't crying for me. She was crying over a man she loved, who wasn't me.

I tell myself it won't work. She will never accept me. The same way my father didn't when he said he fathered an imperfect son. It was why he left. Since then, I've spent my whole life fighting to prove that I'm a man. Being deaf isn't an excuse. I can be a better man and take care of my family. It wasn't their fault I was this way.

I love knowing I'll see her at home when I leave for the day. In my house, she's only a breath away. There are times I forget I'm deaf. She makes me feel normal. Whole.

When I piece together some of Tommy's comments about Ari, I ask Javier what he said. He said her ex- boyfriend's name was Jimmy, the one she cried for at night. I want to know who Jimmy is.

Javier's truck stops at a red light. He is saying something to her. I take out my phone to text Ari.

Rey: Who is Jimmy?

My brother glances at me before the light turns green. I guess he figured out that I texted Ari because she stopped talking.

Ari: My ex-boyfriend. Why?

I watch her expression of lingering unease in the mirror from the visor.

Rey: Who is he exactly?

Ari: My ex-boyfriend is Jimmy Harding. He plays for the Flyers.

Rey: Is he bothering you?

I can tell that he does from the worry that crosses her eyes. The reason she was sleeping in her car.

> Ari: I haven't talked to him since I broke up with him. I won't lie and tell you that he doesn't call me because he does, but it's over between us. I'm sure Tommy will tell him where I'm working. I'm sorry.

I google Jimmy Harding. His picture pops up along with his highlights. He attended Penn State and, like she said, was signed by the Flyers with a hefty contract after completing a year of college. He is blond with light eyes. He reminds me of William Zabka, who played Johnny in part one of *Karate Kid*.

I shift in my seat and show her the screen from my phone. She nods. If I judge the situation by the kiss we shared, it's safe to say she is over him.

> Rey: Do you think he will show up and cause you any trouble?

She can do better. I want to make sure she feels safe. I want her to know that I'll protect her from anyone.

> Ari: I hope not. We didn't leave on the best of terms. I'm sorry about everything today. If it weren't for me, you wouldn't have had to hit Tommy.

> Rey: It's not your fault. I was wrong for how I treated you. Tommy got what he deserved, and by the way, I'm better looking than Jimmy. ;)

> Ari: Fishing for compliments?

> Rey: Maybe.

> Ari: You kiss me better. You need to work on where you put your hands.

My hands?

Rey: I'm glad you agree. Where would you have wanted my hands, Ari?

Ari: Everywhere.

JAVIER AND REY are on their morning run. When I leave the shower, my phone goes off from a text.

> Javier: Hey, Ari. It's Saturday, and I was wondering if you'd like to go out dancing with us.

My stomach churns with a mix of anticipation and dread. The word "us" in Javier's message is a loaded one, implying that Rey will be there too.

> Ari: Where are we going? What should I wear?

> Javier: A dance club. You got a dress?

I do. I was able to get something for my birthday after Jimmy was signed, but he canceled our date at the last minute.

After spending the day getting ready, I styled my hair, painted my nails, and spent over an hour on my makeup. I look at myself in the mirror for the fifth time.

My long, sleek hair cascades down my back, contrasting with the body-hugging dress that accentuates my curves. I adjust the over-the-knee, suede, pointed-toe boots, ensuring they're perfect. I grab a coat, a small wallet, and my phone, ready for the night.

Before I head out, I spray a little perfume.

The pit of my stomach churns with a mix of nerves and anticipation. It's been so long since I've dressed up and gone out dancing.

I take a deep breath to calm my nerves before heading to the living room.

I hear a woman's laugh. Javier didn't mention anyone else. He said…us.

I grip the sleeves of my coat like a shield, and I'm glad it covers my legs and the back of my dress.

"There she is. I was about to call you," Javier says, looking me up and down from head to toe. "You look… amazing."

"Thank you. You look nice, too."

His cheeks flush bright red. "Thank you, Ari."

I look behind him, and my stomach sinks. There is a tall, thin blonde seated close to Rey. Closer than what would be considered friendly.

She smiles at me, and I instantly wish she had warts all over her face. She has blond hair, perfectly shaped lips, and long legs. Her fitted dress hugs every curve of her body.

Rey's eyes avoid mine, and at that moment, I feel the weight of our unspoken connection. My heart sinks, a heavy stone in my chest, as I realize that our relationship is not what I had hoped it to be.

I read too much into last week's kiss. It hasn't happened again, but that doesn't mean I hoped it wouldn't.

"You must be me, Ari," she gushes. "I'm Julia. Javier has told me so much about you. I've known Rey and Javier since I was a senior in high school."

Her voice drips with bubbles and too much champagne. As much as I want to hate her, I have no reason to. She shares a history with him with which I cannot compete.

I can't tear my eyes away from the way she smiles at Rey, a

smile that feels too intimate, too possessive. A surge of jealousy, hot and sharp, pierces through me like a thousand tiny needles.

I give her a fake smile. "So are you and Rey like... together?" I ask, the words coming before I can stop them.

She giggles. Rey blinks.

She glances at Rey and then at me. "We're close," she says, giving me a hopeful smile.

It says a lot. Rey's never mentioned her.

THE DRIVER DROPS us off at an exclusive club near Center City.

As we walk through the dark hallway toward the VIP area, a mix of Spanish, hip-hop, dance, and pop music plays. A large dance area is in the center of the club, and the DJ booth is in the corner. It's dark, with only the lights overhead and the ones under the couches.

I sit next to Javier on the black couch. He invited me so he wouldn't look like the third wheel, and I understand why. Julia has been texting Rey all night because he has been glued to his phone screen, and not once has he sent me a message. I've checked my phone like a lovestruck idiot in the car on the way here. According to Javier, Rey doesn't want anyone to know he is deaf. I know there is more he doesn't tell me, but I don't want to pry.

After fifteen minutes and two shots, the liquid courage has me firing off at Rey.

> Ari: I didn't know you dated?

The light from the phone shines over his face, and his lips form a grim line.

> Rey: Julia is a close friend I met in high school when my mother moved us here from Puerto Rico when I started boxing. We go out sometimes. I didn't think it important to tell you about her.

My heart feels like a fissure in a glass about to shatter. With just one push, it will break into pieces. My hope evaporated like smoke. I haven't taken my coat off because I feel stupid for dressing up for him.

> Ari: It's none of my business.

> Rey: Look, Ari, we had one kiss and a few texts that would be considered flirting. I don't want you to think I'm taking advantage of you.

Javier says something. I nod even though I haven't been listening. I hope he doesn't expect me to answer.

It was a stupid kiss, Ari. It meant nothing.

Julia shifts on the couch. She leans close and surprises Rey with a kiss on the lips. I swallow the bitter taste of hurt on my tongue.

I look away and press send.

> Ari: I understand, and you're right, it was a mistake.

"Is everything alright, Ari?" Javier asks.

I place my phone in my bag. "Yeah"

"Would you dance with me, Ari?" he asks with hopeful eyes and an adorable smile, worried I'd say no.

I slide my hand in his and he helps me stand. Julia and Rey look up.

Julia's mouth is smeared with lipstick.

I grab a small white napkin from the table next to the bottle of champagne, hand it to her, and say, "Javier and I are going to dance."

"I'll see if Rey wants to go, too," she says brightly.

"Good luck with that," Javier says playfully. "You know how Rey feels about dancing."

Javier helps me remove my coat. I adjust the hem of my dress.

"That dress is gorgeous on you, Ari," Julia blurts. "Thank you," I reply politely.

Javier lowers his voice near my ear. "I guess I'm the lucky one tonight." I turn away with a blush. He places his hand on my lower back and guides me to the dance floor.

We dance to a few songs, but he senses the tension. He must feel it.

He leans in and says over the music, "My brother wants you."

"I don't know what you're talking about," I lie, but he must see it because he says, "It's why Julia was all over him. I know something happened between you two."

I play dumb. "What?"

"You looked like I did when a girl broke my heart for the first time. I won't let him do that to you, Ari. He's my brother, and I respect him, but you don't deserve that."

"We kissed," I admit. "It was a mistake. I was surprised when I saw Julia. I felt guilty, but he told me the truth."

He frowns. "I'm sorry, Ari. I didn't know, but it was me...I invited her."

I shrug like it's no big deal. It was Javier who invited her even though deep down, it matters. It matters because it hurts to be rejected.

The music changes. I dance to the beat seductively, trying

to think of anything else while maintaining a respectable distance.

"Where did you learn to dance?" he asks.

I lift my hair and fan myself. "I was on the dance team during high school. We won the state competition four years in a row."

His eyebrows rise, impressed. When he turns us around, I spot Julia with Rey on the edge of the dance floor by the speaker.

Rey looks uncomfortable watching people dance, and Julia awkwardly moves her shoulders. You can tell she isn't a good dancer.

It seems Rey is trying to follow the beat, but Julia's dance moves make it hard for him to find a rhythm.

I look away when he catches me staring. Javier's hands slide to my waist, and he pulls me closer. "My brother doesn't like me dancing with you. I'm sure you are wondering if he can hear the music," he says over my ear. "Since it's so loud, he can pick up the beat or feel the speaker's vibration."

"He can hear the music?" I say, not wanting to ask why he thinks Rey is bothered.

Javier nods. "Yeah, if it's this loud. It's like a soft beat, whispers that fade in and out. I've asked him a bunch of times. It's why he wears headphones when he trains. He plays music as loud as it can go," he says with a smile. "It's better than nothing." I nod in understanding.

That is why he wears the headphones when he works out.

"Will it always be like that?"

Javier shakes his head and says, "One day, it will be gone, Ari. He will wake up and not even hear that."

My heart sinks. That's horrible. He must feel helpless. He will be left in the dark while the world and everything he cares about will move on. To hear and then, one day, silence.

If he waits to have a family, he will never be able to listen to his wife say I do or his baby's first word.

Julia walks up, fanning herself. "Hey guys, I could use another drink."

"I'm okay," I rush out. "I've had enough for the night." She turns to Javier, hopefully. "How about you?"

"I'm good," Javier says.

"At least come with me," she whines.

Javier grins, but he doesn't want to go to the bar. "Are you okay with staying here with Rey until I get back, Ari?"

"Go ahead. I'll be right here."

"Yes," Julia exclaims as if she's won a prize.

They both head to the bar, and I'm left with Rey on the dance floor.

He steps closer to me as the crowd grows thick. A couple bumps me from behind, and I catch myself from falling forward by putting my hands flat on his chest. I feel his muscles twitch underneath. I look up. His eyes dip to where my chest meets his torso. He places his hands on my lower back, and his fingers play with the tips of my hair, causing tingles to snake up my spine.

Relax, Ari.

I look over at Javier and Julia at the bar. Julia laughs and takes shots while snapping selfies as Javier holds her steady. He chuckles at her clumsiness. She laughs louder when she sways, not because of the music.

The DJ saves the day and plays a dance beat, amping up the crowd. I turn away and dance.

When I sneak a glance at Rey over my shoulder, he is looking at my ass with his head tilted to the side. He grips my hips and pulls my back close to his front. His breath on my neck is like fire igniting my skin.

He matches my movements, grinding against me. His hand

slides to my lower stomach and then up slowly to my ribs. Everything fades away until it is just us. Just the feel of his hands on my body. I have to remind myself we are just dancing, but I'm going out of my mind. I try to ignore the tension he creates over my skin. The feel of his hard body on my back. The air from his breath on the back of my neck.

When it's too much, I turn around, and he places his thumb over my beating pulse. It feels like it's running a mile a minute.

He holds me close, tight against him, his nose buried in my hair as I grind my hips.

The song moves to another and then another. After the fourth song, he pauses, scans the other couples, and watches them dance Spanish bachata.

I step slowly to the side so he can follow. In high school, I learned to dance to this from a Dominican girl on the dance team.

His eyes fall to my lips for a few seconds after he catches on. It feels like my heart is beating to a love song.

After a few seconds, a bright light shines overhead. Rey squints. The DJ announces over the mic, "We have royalty from the boxing world with us on the floor tonight, every- one. The Silent King is in the house!"

The crowd erupts in cheers. He realizes he's been spotted but doesn't miss a step. He pulls me closer, sliding my leg between his.

His eyes hold mine when he slides one hand on the side of my neck under my jaw.

My hands are on his shoulders, and we are one. Lost in the magic of the lyrics.

When the song ends, we head back to the VIP area, where we find a drunk Julia pouting playfully at Rey. And I don't think Rey is a fan.

"I should have been dancing with hiiim," she slurs. "I wanted to be picture recorded." She continues incoherently.

Javier shakes his head and laughs.

> Rey: Are you ready to go?

Ari: Yes.

Javier settles the bill with the server. Rey has to guide Julia because she is walking like Bambi in her heels toward the exit. She can hardly keep her eyes open when she is seated in the car.

"Why did you dance with her and not with me?" she slurs, lolling her head to the side.

She's talking to Rey, but I don't think she remembers that he can't hear.

He glances at Javier, and Javier signs. Rey glances at me and then at Javier with a tight expression.

I have learned a bit of ASL in class and studied when I can, but Javier is moving his hands too fast, and I can't follow.

As I watch, I feel a pang of sadness as Rey's arm encircles Julia, her head resting on his shoulder as she sleeps. It is intimate.

Rey's eyes widen with urgency when he notices me watching, but I look away. The tiny light of hope fades into the dark.

ARI

REY PRACTICALLY DRAGS Julia when we walk into his house. She moans something about not wanting to be carried. She pushes at his hand, and for a split second, I wish he would dump her on the floor and leave her to sleep it off. Then I feel awful for thinking this way.

He practically carries her through the house and puts her to sleep. I'm unsure if it's his bedroom or a guest room. I have never been in his room.

I walk toward the kitchen after Javier tells me good night with a peck on the cheek.

Opening the cabinet door, I pull out a packet of popcorn. I can't sleep knowing that Julia is sleeping with Rey. I'll toss and turn, trying to dissect my feelings.

When the popcorn is done, I pour it into a bowl and take a seat in the living room.

I scroll through Netflix and stop on *The Notebook* to wallow in self-pity. I place the popcorn on the coffee table and remove my boots.

I grab the bowl, lift my feet, and then hear a door close, followed by footsteps.

Butterflies swarm like bees in my stomach when Rey plops beside me and pulls his phone out.

Rey: What are you watching?

Ari: The Notebook

He smiles and shakes his head.

Rey: Why do women love that movie?

I frown and turn to him like he's lost his mind.

He gently pushes me back on the couch, careful not to spill the popcorn, and lifts my legs over his lap. He raises his brow and dips his hand in the popcorn.

Ari: Because it's a beautiful story. After years of being apart, he spent a year building a house for her because he believed their love was strong enough to bring her back to him. When she has dementia, he reads her their story so she can remember him. He never leaves her side. And to top it off, they die in each other's arms in old age. What's not to like about it? It's beautiful. It's perfection.

Rey: Is that what you want, Ari? For someone to love you that way?

Ari: Yes, Rey.

Rey: I think you will have to fall in love first.

Ari: Have you ever been in love?

Rey: No.

Ari: Do you want to fall in love?

He glances up at me and then looks back at his phone.

> Rey: I don't think I'm capable. Forgive me
> for not telling you earlier, but you looked
> beautiful tonight. A lot of people
> thought so.

I furrow my brows as I look at the picture he sent through text. It's a photo of us dancing together at the club, posted on social media. The image is captioned, "The King has found his Queen." The comments read, "She's so pretty" and "That dress is gorgeous!" The dress is bad luck. Both times I have worn it for someone, I end up disappointed. Jimmy stood me up and was most likely with someone else. Rey did the same. It's safe to say I should burn it instead of donating it to charity. I would be doing a disservice to the female population. I'm unsure how he feels being seen with me instead of Julia and how people must think we're together.

> Ari: Too bad I'm not going to wear it again.
> It's only brought me bad luck.

> Rey: How come?

> Ari: Both times I've worn it, I ended up
> alone.

> Rey: How's that?

Since breaking up with him, I didn't think I could talk about Jimmy, but I find myself telling Rey anyway.

> Ari: I originally got the dress to celebrate
> when Jimmy signed with the Flyers. It's the
> most expensive dress I own, and I thought
> it would be a special night. It took two
> hours to get ready, and then he called to
> tell me he couldn't make it. I ended up
> watching Netflix until I fell asleep.

Rey: And the second?

Ari: I ended up watching Netflix.

I won't tell him I wore it for him.

Rey: At least you're not alone this time, and
I got to see you in the dress before he did.

I shift on the couch when he puts his phone down.

His hand slides up my bare leg and stops below the hem of my dress. He takes the bowl of popcorn from my hands, along with my cell phone, and places it on the table.

He pulls me toward him to straddle him. Both of his hands slide down the sides of my thighs, shoving my dress up to my waist.

I look down at the scrap of lace covering my pussy when I feel his hand between my thighs.

"And now?" he says hoarsely.

My fingers slide into his hair, and I meet his lips. His hand slides slowly over my ass, pulling me against him. The taste of mint and popcorn fuses to my mouth when he hungrily slides his tongue inside. A small groan escapes his throat when I grind my hips.

I'm breathless when he pushes the strap of my dress over the curve of my shoulder. My right breast peeks out. I undulate my hips.

His eyes burn like flames, and our breaths mingle as we struggle not to lose control. He licks my breasts, sucking and teasing. I close my eyes, arch my back, and move faster.

"You could... never... be... a mistake, Ari," he whispers against my skin, teasing me with the tip of his tongue. His teeth mark my skin.

I can tell he doesn't talk much. The words sound forced like he's learned how to say them recently.

He pulls my nipple out of his mouth when I slide my hands under the hem of his shirt.

He lifts his arms so I can pull it off. His muscles flex. My mouth goes dry at how gorgeous he is. My fingers trace his tattoos over his pecs, and I feel every ridge and groove under my fingers like ripples of sand after the tide.

My hand dips into the waistband of his pants, needing to feel his hard length. He leans back and places his thumb over my clit. My nerves explode, sending electrical pulses to my clit. I can't think. Nothing matters but the need to come.

His eyes are like dark chocolate as he watches me, asking me permission with his eyes when he dips his finger inside me. My fingers slide back up his torso, and I widen my legs to let him. Two fingers slide deep, and his thumb rubs my clit as I bite back the moan wanting to escape. He moves faster, fucking me with his hand. My climax builds like the sun, fire heating my skin, and I melt like a puddle under him.

He kisses my lips softly, then nibbles, holding me with his eyes, and whispers, "You're so..." His words trail off when I fall apart.

My thighs tremble. One hand grips my dress near my hips, his fingers deep inside me, and I'm lost. His voice. Like a precious gift, setting the rhythm to which my heart beats with the magic of his fingers when he licks them clean.

He removes my dress, pulling it up from where it is bunched around my waist, and reaches for his shirt. He places it over my head.

I close my eyes and breathe in his scent. He says he isn't capable of falling in love, but I am hopelessly his.

REY

THE SENSATION of something shakes me, but it stops. Then I feel it again. I don't want to wake up. I feel warm, like I'm on a sandy beach with a blue sky. I can hear her voice and the sound of her laughter. No sadness, guilt, or anyone telling me I'm not good enough. I want to stay in these moments and dream of her and how she smiles. The way she looks at me like I'm everything she's wished for.

Aria.

When my eyes finally open, I squint at the harsh light from the window and see Javier nudging my shoulder.

He points toward my chest, giving me a disappointed look.

I tuck my chin to my chest and see Ari asleep over my bare chest. My eyes follow the lines of her waist to the T-shirt riding up, exposing the soft skin of her thigh, her leg entwined with mine. You can tell she is naked underneath, and the thought has my hands flying to the hem of the shirt, pulling it down from Javier's view.

He shakes his head in response.

I close my eyes and kiss her forehead because it pains me to move from under her. I wish I had taken her to bed, but I didn't want reality to sink in. I wanted her in my arms.

After I safely detach myself from her, Javier asks, "What the fuck? You have Julia in the other room." He pauses, takes a deep breath, and continues. "Tell Julia the truth about Ari. Tell Ari how you feel about her."

I give him a scornful laugh, letting him think I don't care.

He points at the loveseat, where my hoodie, sneakers, and beanie are.

"Get dressed, player," he signs, but I see his lips move. "Stop it," I sign.

"Stop being an asshole."

"You invited her last night," I sign.

"If I would have known about you and Ari, I wouldn't have, but I'm not going to let you hurt them. It's not right, Rey. Tell them."

"I have."

Julia knows how I feel about her. It's his fault for inviting her. I went out with her to make him happy.

"Tell Ari the truth," he signs and then arches a brow, waiting for an answer.

"I can't."

I don't want Julia, but I can't have Ari. I can't build her a dream house or read to her. She doesn't deserve to be with a man who can't hear. I can't hear her cry for help or know what her voice is like. She doesn't deserve that.

"Why?"

"Because I don't love her, and I never will," I lie.

"Then don't lead her on."

"You're right," I sign. "I can't be what she wants."

"Then why were you with her last night?"

"Because I'm a man." But I can tell he doesn't believe that is the reason.

"Are you falling for Ari, Rey?"

He wants me to bare my fucking heart. Wanting someone and loving them are two different things. Sex is easy and uncomplicated. Love is complicated and promises forever. I can't give her forever when there is a huge barrier between us called silence. I have to do the right thing, even if it feels wrong. I'm tired of robbing people of the quality of life they should have had because of me.

"No. I'm not falling in love with Ari," I sign, feeling my hands break when I see his expression turn to sadness, and I know she's awake. I can feel her.

A sickening feeling pools in my stomach like I drank poison.

I turn around, watching her grab her phone and clothes, and hate myself when I see her run up the stairs.

I should run after her, but I'm afraid of seeing the disappointment on her beautiful face.

Last night, I saw the way men gave her appreciative glances. I hated that I didn't have control. I hated the look on her face when Julia kissed me, and it tore me apart when she saw her on my shoulder.

I don't want Ari to think I slept with Julia when she is the one I want.

When I turn around, Julia has a murderous look in her eyes. Her phone is in her hand, and she's throwing her hands up. Thick, messy globs of last night's mascara are under her eyes like a bad Halloween makeup job.

Javier looks at me and then at Julia as she rants. But all I can think about is Ari and what she must be thinking.

Did Ari understand what I said? She couldn't have because Ari doesn't know ASL.

Julia never bothered to learn in all the years I've known her. She said learning ASL is pointless when there are cell phones, and she covered up her reason by saying people would look. They would know the secret I kept from the world. I guess she was right, but sometimes it's easier to sign than text.

Julia: I can't believe you, Rey. It is all over social media. Have you seen the pictures of you with her? How you were holding her. Everyone thinks you two were together when you were there with me. How could you do this to me? I'm humiliated. I posted pictures of us to all my friends and on my page last night. It is always the same with you, Rey. I love you. I have loved you since I was in high school. I have waited for you. I have been there for you.

Julia: Are you sleeping with her? You didn't sleep with me last night.

I look up, and tears stream heavily down her cheeks.

Her lips move, and she asks, "Did you?"

I grab my hoodie, annoyed with her for asking. I'm too busy tormented by the thought of Ari watching Julia kiss me last night and wondering if she understood the lie I spilled to Javier.

"I hate you," she mouths as more tears cast down her face.

I look down at my phone and send her a text.

Rey: I'm sorry, Julia. I'm sorry I can't be what you want and never will.

Julia: Do you love her?

I only saw her as a friend who liked to have casual sex.

Rey: Javier was wrong to invite you. I'm sorry, but I gotta go.

She shakes her head in disappointment. Javier tries to help her collect her things, but she shrugs him off and says something to him I can't read from her lips.

We both watch her stomp through the house in her heels as she walks out the door.

Javier gives me a grim expression and signs, "I hate to be you right now, but I think you did the right thing."

"What did she say when she left?"

"She said she hoped Ari would break your heart like you just broke hers."

I have never been afraid of a fight in my entire life, but a sexy five-foot-four brunette with a gorgeous face and a sexy body scares the shit out of me.

When I'm with her, I forget that I'm the undefeated heavyweight champion of the world. Because to her, I'm just Rey. And to me, she is the perfect storm I never saw coming. She doesn't need a picture with me to show off. She doesn't care about social media or what other people think. She wants her Noah.

After Javier leaves for his run, I tell him I'll meet him outside, but I find myself sitting on the couch scrolling through Jimmy's social media page. Every picture he has posted is of himself playing hockey. Highlights and a few with Ari. I hate to admit that I stalked his IG for twenty minutes. I wanted to see what she saw in him. Why did they break up?

I swipe through his recent pictures and pause when I see him at a bar with several celebrity hockey players from his team. I notice a blond girl with her hand on his lap leaning close. She isn't prettier than Ari. Not even close. Ari has thick, straight hair. Plump lips where the top is slightly bigger than the bottom, begging for a kiss. Her nose is small, with a little swoop on its bridge. An innocence you want to protect. A body you want to unravel.

He cheated on her.

She thinks I used her and would do the same.

After my run, I find Ari in the kitchen making something to eat.

She smiles at Javier, and my chest hurts because I can see the hurt pulsing in her eyes. I can feel the tension between us in the room.

When she turns around, Javier signs, "Stop staring at her."

"I wasn't," I sign back.

He rolls his eyes and glances at Ari. She quirks her brow when she places three plates on the table. Javier gives her a white-toothed smile because the food smells delicious. She made one of our approved meals I left by the kitchen.

When she turns around, he signs, "You were staring at her ass."

"Maybe, I like her ass. There are a lot of things I like about her. Her ass is one of them, and besides, she wasn't complaining last night when my hands were all over her ass, and don't let me catch you checking her out."

He smirks. "Funny. I really do hope she busts your balls wide open. I hope she breaks your heart."

"I don't have a heart. I'm not you, Javier," I sign, immediately wanting to take what I said back.

He glares at me and throws a spoon at me for mentioning that he had his heart broken when he was a senior in high school.

Ari comes to the breakfast table, places her hands on her hips, and stares down at me while I sip water.

She starts signing, and I almost choke. "I know you don't want me, but Javier's right, stop staring at my ass. We need to discuss setting boundaries if you still want me to work for you. If you want me to leave, I can do that too. Let me know. The homeless shelter fills up quickly after two."

Javier has his fork in the air, his mouth hanging open. He

says something to her, and she nods and then moves her head from side to side.

When did she learn how to sign?

Javier looks up at me and answers, "She signed up for ASL class as an elective at the beginning of her last semester. She has been practicing and watching videos to learn how to communicate through sign language since her boss is deaf. She knows about two hundred and twenty-five words."

She picks up her phone and sends me a voice message before she gets up and leaves the room.

Ari: Javier said you could hear some if it is loud enough.

I grab the headphones from the clinic and press play on my phone. Her voice is faint, but I hear it. I close my eyes so I don't miss a word. The soft tone of her voice causes my heart to beat faster, like watching a baby take its first steps—memorable.

"Umm…if you can hear me, this is my voice. I did this after you fell asleep last night and hoped it works. I wanted you to hear what I sounded like. You gifted me the sound of your voice, and I wanted to give you mine. My last name is Jensen, but you already know that because I work for you. I will repeat your name so you can hear me say it, Rey Vicente. I know it means king in Spanish; hence, it's your ring name, but I don't think you're silent. I think you have a beautiful voice that matches a man I have come to admire. If you can tell, one that I like very much. I know things are complicated. I know a lot is going on in your life. You are losing something precious and will never get it back. Since some of it is still here, make the most of it. I don't want to talk about serious relationships or want you to think I expect more from you." She laughs nervously and continues. "So who's a better kisser? Me or Julia?"

I don't deserve her. Her voice is beautiful. "Oh, and for the record, the greatest love story is never written, Rey. It is lived. I hope you live yours with someone special someday. I want to tell you a little about myself. My father was born in Pennsylvania, and my mother is from Panama. I speak Spanish; I like dancing to all types of music. I also like pasta; my favorite color is black because it goes with everything. I don't want to bore you, but I wanted to let you know that I like my job, and thank you for giving me a place to stay until I get back on my feet. Gracias, por todo."

The recording ends. I open my eyes. A tear falls down my cheek. I got to hear her voice and her laughter. I got to listen to the way she said my name.

I'm terrified the day she leaves because I've said words I can't take back.

> Rey: You kiss better. It will always… be
> you. You can still be with me as long as you
> need.

REY

ARI AND JAVIER are in the kitchen, cleaning the dishes. I didn't ask her to. I don't want them to do it together, but Javier insists on helping.

The recessed lights flash purple, letting me know someone is at the gate. My phone vibrates in my front pocket. I pause the footage of Javier's opponent's last fight and get up from the couch to check the camera. It's my mother.

I look over my shoulder. Ari is smiling at something Javier said. There are times I imagine that I can hear her talking to my brother about a trip we took for a vacation, how much she loved it, how we plan to go to a cabin in the mountains next month, and where we will have Thanksgiving.

I watch Javier's head lift as he hears my mother coming through the front door. His face breaks out into a big smile. Ari's gaze lands on mine, and her eyes widen slightly. I see her hands fidget with the dish towel placed on the counter.

My mother places a hand on my shoulder, and I turn to meet her soft brown eyes, which are full of warmth. I give her a warm smile. My eyes tell her that I've missed her.

My mother is one of the most important people in my life. She has sacrificed so much for me and always chose us. She never remarried. She never took another chance at love, and I understand why. She gave a man two sons, and when it got hard because one of them wasn't born perfect, he abandoned her. He abandoned us. She is one of the bravest women I have ever met. The second is walking over and kissing my mother's cheek as a greeting. My mother steps back, holding Ari's hands. She takes a good look and smiles with approval. She glances at me and my brother, and I can see the matchmaking wheel turning in her eyes.

She sits across from me and waits until Ari returns to the kitchen.

"She is gorgeous," she signs.

"She works for us in the office at the gym. And yes, I know. She's staying with us for a while until she finds an apartment."

My eyes follow Ari while she dries the last of the dishes, and Javier puts the others away.

When I turn around to pick up the remote and hit play, my mother signs, "You like her. I can see it when you look at her."

When I don't respond, my mother raises her eyebrows.

I sigh. "She's the serious relationship type. She wants a man like Noah from *The Notebook*."

"You are no Noah. You're better looking with a good heart. I have faith in you, Rey. I can tell she would be perfect for you. Javier seems to get along with her very well. She is polite. She obviously helps you boys around the house. I don't see the problem."

"Trust me, Mom. I know, but I'm the problem. There is nothing wrong with Ari."

I pick up my phone. She pulls hers out of her handbag for privacy. I tell her everything that happened last night without the details of what I did to her on the couch.

Mom: You are saying that because you hurt her and feel guilty. I hate to say this, but I'm disappointed in you, Rey. I didn't raise you boys like that. You're right. You should leave her alone. Let someone else be her Noah.

Isn't this what I wanted? For Ari to see that I'm no good for her. Then why do I feel like I've lost the biggest fight of my life? Even my mother knows I've ruined my chances with Ari.

Javier and Ari return from the kitchen. Javier takes a seat next to my mother. Ari glances at me on the couch, and my heart sinks. She sits on a single chair as far away from me as possible.

Ari says something to my mom, but my gaze is fixed on her. I know it's only a matter of time before she leaves.

ARI

THERE IS one more month until Javier's fight. I'm excited but nervous for him at the same time. He has been training with Rey nonstop, at home and in the gym, six days a week. I have been helping them prepare their meals at home.

It has been difficult keeping my distance from Rey. It's hard not to look at him when he's shirtless in the ring training with Javier. His skin glistens under the lights like a mirror, and the way the sweat drips down his muscled chest. He's all I can think about and the cause of the heat between my legs when I'm alone in my room, replaying that night. How right and wrong it was, and how it could never happen again.

Their mother is amazing. As soon as she walked into the house, I could tell that the loves of her life were in the room. Rey has a special bond with his mother. His admiration for her can be felt like the sun's warmth in the room.

My phone rattles on the wooden desk, causing the pens to pop like popcorn. When it goes off, I pick it up with a frown.

> Jimmy: I miss you, Ari. I want you to know that I'm thinking of you.

He must be bored.

> Jimmy: I hope you are doing okay. I'm lost without you. I made a mistake, and I'm sorry. I told Mandy I'm in love with you. Despite what you might think, I do love you, Ari. Don't throw us away.

I doubt he felt this way when he was screwing her?

It's been a while since he texted me. I mentally count a month and three weeks since his previous rant. I know there will be more, and on cue, the pens on the desk rattle from my phone going off.

> Jimmy: I heard you were working at a boxing gym. I hope they are treating you right. If you need money, Ari, you could ask me.

> Jimmy: Could you text me back so I know you're okay? I checked the dorms, and you aren't listed. I called your parents, but they hung up on me after they said they didn't know where you were staying.

Shit, that's why my mother called during class the day before yesterday. I told my parents the truth about Jimmy but lied about returning to the dorm.

> Jimmy: I don't know where you are staying, but I hope it's safe. Please, Ari, answer me. I worry about you.

I shake my head. He must think I'm stupid or something. This needs to stop. He needs to let the idea of me going back go.

Ari: Stop texting me, Jimmy. I'm trying to
work. I haven't answered you because
we're done. I have nothing to say to you.
We're over.

I drop my phone after hitting send, and then it vibrates again. I pick it up, about to block Jimmy's number, when I see it's from Rey.

Rey: Is everything okay?

I look up, and he is leaning his shoulder on the doorjamb. His massive arms are folded over his shirtless chest, covered in sweat, and his cell phone is in his hand.

Ari: Everything is fine.

It isn't. I'm tired of being used and rejected, of not being able to make it alone. I'm tired of having to depend on someone to survive and not be good enough for someone to want me.

Rey: Are you sure? You looked upset. Is
something or someone bothering you?

It's not your problem—I'm not your problem. But I don't say it, I have to keep boundaries in place. I've avoided him as much as possible. I don't sit close, and I avoid being alone with him at all costs. He's my boss; I'm his employee. He's made it clear there can be nothing between us.

Ari: I'm not upset. Thank you for asking,
Rey. Did you need anything?

Rey: Is your ex bothering you?

Rey: Tell him I don't like that he's still
calling you.

Ari: If he was, I wouldn't tell him that. I
don't like lying.

I hate lying to him, but Jimmy is my problem.

I place my phone in my purse, but it goes off when he walks out.

Rey: Who said you were lying?

I'M FINALLY CAUGHT up on filing. Each member signed up at the gym has all their waivers and required forms signed and updated.

I slide the drawer closed with my hip when there is a knock on the door.

I look up, and my face falls when I see Jimmy.

"Hey," he says with a small smile, giving me a once-over.

"What are you doing here, Jimmy?" I ask in a hard tone.

He slides a hand into his pocket. "I wanted to see if you had a minute?"

"I'm working."

"I know. I..." He pauses like he's mincing his words. This is borderline stalking. When I was leaving class, one of my professors said he came around looking for me in his earlier class. Apparently, Jimmy doesn't know what time my classes are but knows my schedule.

He walks farther into the office, and I can't help but notice that he hasn't shaved in a couple of days. His eyes are red-rimmed. He looks like he hasn't slept. Frankly, he looks like shit.

"Why are you here?"

"I didn't come here to fight."

"That I do believe because boxing isn't your sport."

He doesn't reply. Instead, he takes a seat in the chair in

front of my desk. "Sure, go ahead, make yourself right at home, Jimmy."

"I want you to come home, Ari."

I laugh and rub my eyes, hoping this is a bad dream, and I'll wake up and find him gone.

I blink several times, but he's still watching me with a hopeful expression, hoping I'll fall for it. He wanted me to go back because it was convenient for him. He was comfortable with our arrangement because I didn't question him. I never asked him for more or pressured him to give me more.

"Your home is not my home. It never was. My answer is no, and it will continue to be no."

He slides forward, placing his hands on the desk. "Of course, my home is your home. It's our home."

He says the last part, and it sounds like nails on a chalk-board. The look in his eyes is borderline obsessive, and it's not the good kind.

"Well, last time I was there, it was a little crowded. It's not my style." I want him to go. He can't mess up this job for me. Rey and Javier don't need this right now. I don't need this right now. I can't move forward with my past constantly showing up. "I need you to leave."

A large shadow slides across the desk. Rey stands at the door, glaring at Jimmy. His eyes find mine, and he is giving me the "what the fuck is he doing here" look.

I shake my head, telling him to let me handle it. Jimmy notices my attention is on something behind him.

He takes one look at Rey and stands up. "Of course." He points between me and Rey and squares up. Rey is double his size, but Jimmy is a hard-ass. He doesn't back down. "You fucking my girl?"

"Jimmy!" I warn. "You need to leave," I demand.

"Save it, Ari," he says to me, but his eyes are on Rey. "I'm not stupid. I saw the picture of you two online." Of course, he did. I'm sure many people have. I've pushed it to the back of my mind like it never happened because we aren't together.

Rey stares Jimmy down and steps farther into the room. "Don't, Rey," I mouth slowly.

Javier comes inside to see what is holding Rey up from going back into the ring with his gloves on. "Ari, is every- thing okay?" he asks but quickly sees the problem when he notices Jimmy and Rey are toe-to-toe. "Hey, man. I don't know why you're here, but we don't have time for this."

Jimmy shakes his head. "He"—he points at Rey—"needs to understand that she's my girl, and I'm here to take her home... where she belongs. She doesn't need to work here because I can care for her." He gets closer to Rey, his nose almost touching his chin. "My home," he growls.

Rey's nostrils flare. Tension radiates off the walls, and testosterone is released like a mist in his hair.

"Jimmy, you're going to get me fired."

I don't think Rey and Javier would, but I would get canned if I was working somewhere else.

"Good. I hope he fires you."

"It's over, Jimmy. We're over. There is nothing you can do that will change that. There is nothing you can say to convince me to take you back, and I like working here. I've told you this a hundred times."

Jimmy ignores me, staring at Rey, hoping for a reaction. "What? You're not going to tell me anything? You're just going to stand there and not say shit."

Jimmy steps away, and I flinch when he reaches for me, but Rey grabs Jimmy's arm like lightning before he reaches me and shoves him.

"That's enough," Javier says, standing between Jimmy and Rey. "Hey, man, you need to go. I'm not going to ask again."

Rey steps aside, grabs my hand, and pulls me out of the room. He pushes me gently against the wall outside the office, not caring if people are watching.

He lowers his lips to my ear. "I'm not... going to disrespect you." He swallows. "And tell him what he wants to hear," he says, pausing to take a deep breath. "It is none of his business..." He trails off, grimacing like he's in pain. "Please tell me... please tell me he didn't touch you, Ari." He leans forward and presses a kiss to my forehead. "Please," he rasps. "Please tell me if he's hurt you." He closes his eyes. My heart twists into pieces, trying not to break apart. "Because I won't be able to control myself. I'm not per—I'm no good... for you"—his lips press softly near my ear—"but I'll... protect you."

He steps back when Jimmy leaves the office, tugging me behind him.

Jimmy walks out but then whirls around.

"Hey, man," Javier says, "I'm not going to ask again."

"I still love you, Ari!" he yells, causing everyone in the gym to look over. "He doesn't... but I do. Don't throw us away. He doesn't love you. Guys like him don't love girls like you."

I look at my feet, knowing there is truth in what he is saying, but neither does Jimmy.

Rey turns around and points at the office. Once I'm inside, he shuts the door and whips out his phone. He must be upset about Jimmy showing up. Everyone heard what he said, even if Rey didn't. Now, everyone is going to know that Rey and I are involved.

Rey: Come with me.

Ari: Where?

I look up, confused.

Rey: Anywhere. As long as it's with you.

Ari: Why?

Rey: Because I want to.

Ari: Dressed like that?

He looks at his naked chest, his shorts and sneakers, then types in his phone.

If he plans to take me out to dinner dressed like that, I don't think we'll make it without me jumping all over him in the car.

Rey: Give me a few minutes.

He walks out, leaving me with my conflicting thoughts.

Javier walks in with a worried look in his eyes. "Are you okay?"

I take a deep breath and let it out. "Yeah."

"Ari, is this the first time?"

I avert my gaze, not wanting to admit the truth. The calls. Him showing up at school. The desperate look in Jimmy's eyes. It's like he's waiting for the right time.

Everyone at school knows Jimmy. They think he is a god since he went pro. He buys them drinks at the bar and gives off the nice-guy persona. He doesn't show the monster he can be that I didn't realize lived underneath. The way he looked at the bathroom door that day, making sure Mandy didn't hear the threat in his tone after he shoved me.

Fear swirls in my gut of what might have happened if she wasn't there, and I tried to leave. In a way, I'm glad it ended the way it did. What if I wanted to leave Jimmy because I didn't think we were good together anymore? What if I tried to go, and he turned violent?

"He calls, but I don't answer."

"How many times?"

I wince. "Almost all the time," I say in a soft voice.

He steps forward and lowers his voice. "Does Rey know?"

I shake my head. "I didn't think he would show up here. I've told Jimmy numerous times we're over."

"You need to report him, Ari. That's stalking and harassment."

"Who would believe me, Javier? I'm not stupid. It's my word against theirs. People would think it's harmless."

"Did he hit you? The day we met. Your shoulder?"

I look at my shoes when I notice Rey standing behind him so he won't see my lips. "Please don't tell Rey. He... shoved me the day I left. I came home early to the house and found him walking out of the shower with another girl wearing my robe. It's why I was at the dollar store. I obviously didn't have money and was buying body wash and deodorant."

"Damn, Ari," Javier says.

Rey lifts my chin and looks directly at me. I can see the worry in his eyes. He knows I said something to upset Javier. Something he doesn't know. Something I don't want him to know.

A lone tear slides down my cheek, not because of Jimmy but because of the situation. I know Rey would have hurt him if I told him. He would have sacrificed himself, but I can't let him. I can't be the cause of someone getting hurt because of me.

He wipes the tear from my cheek with his thumb.

Javier clears his throat. "I'll leave you two. If you need anything, Ari, let me know. I'm here if you want to talk."

Rey can sense Javier talking to me but doesn't turn to read

his lips. He watches me, and I wish he could tell me what is going through his mind right now, but I know it will lead me to tell him the truth.

Javier walks out, shutting the door behind him. His mouth lifts in a panty-melting smile. He shoots a quick text and moves to lock the office door.

Rey: I want to talk to you, Ari. Alone.

I adjust my gym hoodie over my leggings and walk over to where he's standing near the edge of the desk. He bends, but instead of whispering, he grabs the hem of my sweatshirt and pulls it up. My arms automatically lift, and he pulls it over my head.

My eyebrows pinch in confusion. He said he wanted to talk, but his gaze travels over my black tank top and stops at the swell of my breasts.

He slides his fingers under the shoulder straps and pulls them down. I'm not wearing a bra, and I watch his eyes, the color of butterscotch, darken when they land on my hard nipples. The memory of the other night when his tongue languidly stroked and teased. Sucked and kissed.

His eyes dip between us. I watch his hand fall to the crotch of his sweatpants, and he adjusts himself.

His hand cups the back of my neck, bringing me close to the space between his neck and shoulder. My nipples brush the fabric of his sweater. I inhale the scent of his freshly showered skin mixed with his cologne.

The evidence of his arousal pushes against my stomach. The backs of his fingers caress my shoulder down to the side of my breasts. I exhale as a thousand nerve endings cause tiny pulses over the skin. My hands find his shoulders when his fingers trail toward the center of my chest, right over my frantically beating heart. I look up and meet his eyes. Rey doesn't express himself with words. It isn't the way he tells me how he feels. It isn't the way I tell him how I feel.

He closes his eyes. A knot forms in my throat as he takes a steady breath. I feel the tiny flutter of his fingers over my beating heart.

It allows me a moment to memorize every feature of his face. His square jaw. His nose. The shape of his eyes. Every scar he received from every fight. The shape of his mouth. The tiny cleft in his chin.

When his eyes open, I want to stay like this forever. In his arms while he listens to the beating of my heart. The way it beats for him.

REY

I'VE NEVER DESIRED a woman the way I desire Ari. When her sleazy ex was near her, all I could think of was getting her away from him. I could see the fear in her eyes when she looked at him. An uneasy feeling crept up my spine. My fighter's intuition tells me he has physically hurt her in the past, which is why she was afraid of me that day with Tommy, but she didn't want to tell me. Knowing Ari, she won't tell me because it's her way of protecting me from what I'll do to him.

I told her I wanted to talk.

This is me talking.

I breathe in the sweet smell of her shampoo from her hair and feel the fast beat of her heart under my fingers. The softness of her skin when I caress her breasts calms me but awakens something else. The need to have her and not let her go.

Her body language. The rhythm of her heart. The fanning of her breath on my skin. She tells me all I need to know. She needs me right now and I'll be here for her.

With every touch on her skin, I can hear the whispers of her soul. With every look I give her, I hope she can hear mine.

———

Movement coming from the top of the stairs catches my eye, and I smile when I see Ari dressed in a beautiful white dress with a black overcoat, black pantyhose, and black pointed pumps coming down the stairs. She looks stunning. Her hair is down just the way I like it.

I think my heart skips a beat when she signs, "You look gorgeous all dressed up."

"Nothing compares to how you look, Ari," I sign.

She blushes, and I give her my arm. I'm impressed she has learned to sign so fast. There are times when she gets stuck. She pauses, sends me a text, and I show her.

When the garage door opens, I grab the keys to the McLaren Javier insisted I buy. I open the door for her, and she slides in. When I slide in on the driver's side, I can't help myself. I lean over the center console. I grip her chin, ignoring the look of surprise across her face, and kiss her gently, pressing my lips to hers.

The kiss is soft and sticky. She tastes like cherries and mint, and...her.

My hand slides around her neck to deepen the kiss. My tongue slides inside her mouth, devouring her, not caring if I get lip-gloss all over my mouth.

I love how she feels and tastes, but we will never make it to dinner if I don't stop now. When we pull apart, she's breathless. My eyes tell her more than words ever could. I want more but could never tell her.

"What about boundaries?" she signs.

"There are no rules when it comes to you."

After the twenty-minute drive to the small restaurant, we are shown to a small, intimate table in the corner. I help remove her coat and can't help but stare at how beautiful she looks.

The server comes up to our table. An older woman in her fifties smiles at us both. I try not to make it obvious that I cannot understand a word she is saying. Ari listens and scans the menu, laying it flat on the table. She points at the beverage section. I tap over the wine bottle section, and she orders a Riesling.

When the server leaves, we settle on what we will order. I pick up my phone.

> Rey: Thank you for ordering.

> Ari: Thank you for taking me out to dinner
> tonight after everything with Jimmy earlier.

> Rey: It's my pleasure. Thank you for
> letting me.

I love the way I make her blush. The way her eyes sparkle under the lights.

> Rey: What are your plans after you
> graduate?

I've been meaning to ask. All I know is that she is in her last semester and will graduate with a degree in human resources.

> Ari: I'm going to start looking. I haven't
> decided where. I'm unsure if I should stay
> in Pennsylvania or move down South,
> where it's warmer. I know how it feels
> sleeping in my car in the cold when you
> can't afford heat.

The memory of that night broke me, but the thought of her leaving felt like a punch to my gut. My stomach turned at the thought of her moving far away. I knew she wouldn't continue working at the gym after she graduated. She deserves to find a job that would make her happy, but I dread the day she tells me she is leaving or moving out because she finds an apartment. I could have offered her money to find a place, but the thought of her moving out doesn't sit well with me. It is selfish of me, but moving into an apartment when she can live with me for free wouldn't make sense. I like her in my house. I want her to work in the gym, where I can sneak a glance when she is lost in thought. When the sun sets, the light causes a glow around her face.

> Rey: You could stay with me as long as you want, Ari.

You don't have to leave after you graduate.

> Ari: I thought you didn't like the idea that Javier hired me.

I smile.

> Rey: You grew on me.

> Ari: How is your mom? She hasn't stopped by since the last time. I could tell you three are close, and she is a good mother who raised her sons well.

> Rey: Thank you. She is on a cruise to the Bahamas with her friends from bingo.

> Ari: Where is your dad?

> Rey: I don't know. He kind of ditched us when I was a kid.

> Ari: I'm sorry.

> Rey: It's okay. I turned out alright, I guess.

> Ari: A little grumpy but not too bad.

I look up and see her playful smile as she waits for my reply.

Rey: How about your parents?

Ari: They live four hours away.
Overprotective but good and hardworking.

Rey: Overprotective how?

Ari: I couldn't date in high school. I couldn't
go out with friends. They had to come over
to my house and only could when my
parents were there.

Rey: How did you meet the hockey player?

I don't want to say his name. He rubs me the wrong way, and the fact I know he's hurt Ari makes me want to put him through a wall after I break his face.

Ari: Freshman year of college. We met at a
party. We were together for three years,
and I made the mistake of moving in with
him last year.

Rey: What happened?

I brace myself for the answer. I have an idea of what to expect, but I want confirmation. I want to know what I'm dealing with if he shows back up. If my intuition is correct, he will not leave her alone. I think he's obsessed with getting her back for all the wrong reasons.

Ari: I came home early and caught him red-
handed walking out of our bathroom with a
girl named Mandy wearing my robe.

The guy must be high and need his brain examined.

Rey: Ouch. I hope you didn't keep the
robe.

Ari: I didn't. Grabbed what I could without a
second thought and left.

Rey: What else happened?

She looks up for a few seconds. Turmoil swirls in the depths of her eyes. I know there is more, but I want more details.

Ari: When I tried to leave to push past him,
he shoved me, and I fell, hitting my
shoulder on the corner of the dresser. He
wasn't sorry and threatened me. When he
was distracted, I ran out of the house and
have avoided him ever since.

Rey: He's obviously stalking you, Ari. Is he
threatening you?

Ari: He wants me to return to him. I've told
him numerous times that we are over.

Rey: Do you love him?

I don't know why I asked her that, but I want to know. I want to know I'm not kissing her when she still loves him, even if he's a lying piece of shit who deserves a fist to his face.

Ari: No. I thought I did, but I didn't.

Rey: You shouldn't be. It's not your fault he
couldn't see what was right in front of him.

Ari: What is that?

Rey: The perfect woman.

She looks up from her phone; her eyes are glassy, tears threatening, and I wonder what I could have said that caused it. What could I have said that is tearing my insides as I watch a wave of sadness fill her eyes?

My phone vibrates in my hand like a tiny earthquake. The words on my screen are like daggers splitting me open, leaving me bleeding.

Ari: If I was, why do I feel like I'm not good enough for anyone?

————

After dinner, I'm on the couch scrolling through Netflix, thinking of the last thing she said before the server came out with our food. The rest of the night was silent. Something I was used to, but I'm sure she wasn't. The night was stiff and empty except for small smiles and polite nods. It wasn't what I had planned. I wanted her to have a nice time with me. After a chaste kiss on the cheek and her signing good night when we reached the garage door threshold, I couldn't sleep. I took a cold shower, and when I closed my eyes, all I saw was the look on her face that night at the club with Julia. It was the same look that crossed her face tonight.

The way her eyes dimmed when she placed her phone down to eat. There was nothing I could say when what I said hung over us like a black cloud.

When I called her the perfect woman, she didn't believe me. The doubt crept in, infecting her beautiful mind. It made me feel less than a man. Unworthy of her.

I wasn't good enough for someone like her. I knew it the day I first saw her. She didn't fit my ugly world.

I had no idea the man she was running away from caused her so much hurt that she found herself lost in the cold, alone for someone like me to find her.

He chose someone else when he had her, and she thought I would do the same. But in my mind, I could never have a woman like Ari. We didn't fit together and never would.

I was destined for a life of silence, and she was destined for all the beautiful possibilities the world had to offer. I hurt her in trying to protect her from heartache. Because all I could give her, in the end, was pain and disappointment.

A man with an impairment. A man who his own father didn't want because he was less than what was considered normal. Damaged. Weak.

It was what I had feared since I was twelve. That one day, everyone around me would see me as a broken man and look at me with pity.

I wouldn't be able to listen to her moans when I'm making love to her. Hear her wants and desires in the spur of the moment. I couldn't talk with her in the car on the way to the mountains on vacation. Hear her sing her favorite song. It was like snuffing out a candle when you were addicted to the scent.

My fingers stopped on the movie she wanted to watch the other night. I kissed her while it was playing, wishing for a split second that she could see me as her Noah, a man from a book who would do anything for the one he loved. I knew I couldn't be what she wanted, but that didn't stop me.

I wanted to feel her come apart in my arms. Feel the shudders that wracked her body. The way she trembled in my arms when I kissed her skin. I shouldn't have touched her or let it get that far, but I couldn't resist her.

But I had to break her heart and obliterate feelings because that is what I did. I wouldn't be able to live with myself if the person I loved one day would wake up and regret being with me because I was different. If it got too hard, and the scales tipped ever so slightly to one side more than the other.

The blue light flickers from the recessed lighting, signaling that someone is walking through the house. I don't have to turn around to know it's her. I can smell her scent. The strawberry-scented lotion I have seen her rub on her skin in the office.

She sits next to me on the couch. I'm looking directly at the screen, but I can feel her gaze on my skin. Her strawberry scent fills my nose, pulling me deeper into her orbit. She shifts on the couch to face me.

"Are we going to finish watching it?" she signs.

I play dumb. "What?"

I know she means *The Notebook*, but I don't want her to know I was thinking about that night, complicating things between us.

One day, she will tell me she has found a job somewhere else in another state, and I will never see her again.

It's for the best. Ari deserves to follow her dreams and accomplish her goals.

"*The Notebook*. Are we going to finish watching it?"

My eyes flick back to the screen. I pick up the remote and try not to look at the way her white tank top stretches over her perky breasts. I nod and press play.

I watch the screen, and out of courtesy, I increase the volume, but she stops me, placing her hand over mine. Her dainty fingers press the button, removing the sound and leaving the subtitles.

She shakes her head playfully and signs, "I think it's better this way."

After twenty minutes, I watch her fall asleep from the

corner of my eye. I should wake her and tell her to go to bed, but I can't.

A little longer, I tell myself.

Just a little longer won't hurt.

When the movie ends, I can't bring myself to move her. Her body is curled up next to me, her head on my chest, and her soft and beautiful hair spread out like a bird's wings.

ARI

MY PIECE of crap car almost left me stranded again. I can't afford to take it to a mechanic. It's still making a horrible noise when I pull in the parking lot of the boxing gym.

The guys passing by and entering the gym give me worried looks. I shrug, thinking it's not my fault my car wants to sound like it's dying when, in fact, it is my fault because I'm broke.

When I get out, the cold air bites my skin, and I act like I know what I'm doing when I lift the hood. I know nothing about fixing cars. I cannot afford to buy myself a car in better condition, and getting this one fixed is not worth it either. I saved enough to get a small apartment.

I look at the rusty engine, not knowing what does what. I am still determining where the noise is coming from exactly.

"Shit," I mutter.

A guy I've seen train with Rey a couple of times walks over. "Hey, do you want me to take a look? It sounded pretty awful when you pulled in."

"That's okay. It's on its last leg, anyway. I think it's past fixing."

He adjusts the strap of his bag over his shoulder. I don't remember his name off the top of my head.

"Ari, right?"

Shit. He knows mine. I smile. "Yeah."

"My name is Chase." He nudges his head toward the

entrance of the gym. "Let's go inside before we freeze to death out here. Even the car can feel it."

I laugh and close the hood. He holds the door open to let me through and asks, "You go to Penn State, right?"

I watch him take off his beanie and ruffle his dark blond hair. He removes his coat while I remove my gloves.

I turn my head and see Rey in the ring with another fighter. He isn't training because he's staring directly at me. His jaw is tense.

The night Rey invited me to dinner, I admitted things I shouldn't and said things that I shouldn't have said.

I was vulnerable. Nervous. I've never had a man who wasn't Jimmy take me out for dinner, and it usually involved going out with his friends.

It was safe to say Jimmy never took me out, just the two of us. It seems he wanted someone to always be there as a witness.

The rest of the night was awkward. I didn't know what to expect. I felt inexperienced and naive when I'm sure he's gone on dates with countless women.

When I heard him in the living room after I changed and was getting ready for bed, I wanted to make things right again between us. I wanted him to know that we were still friends and that I didn't expect more. That we could go on like nothing happened. It was just a few kisses and a lot of rubbing on my part.

That's why I'm desperately looking for an apartment. I have to keep my distance from Rey. I'm the problem. To him, I'm a bird with a broken wing that needed to heal before being set free.

"What year?"

I look up at Chase's voice, returning to the present.

"Oh, um... one more semester, and I will graduate."

"How about you?"

"I graduated last year. I was on the boxing team and then went to the Olympics." My eyebrows rise in surprise. "Now I'm here to train with the best."

"That's impressive, Chase. Rey is the best. You're in good hands if you're part of his team. Anyone watching him with Javier can tell he knows how to train a champion."

"You like him, don't you?"

My cheeks heat, hoping he can't see the truth. I remove my jacket and place it on the coatrack, then walk toward the office. "What do you mean?"

He follows me and says, "Rey. You like him?"

"He's my boss."

I set my bag down on the desk. "When you say his name, your face lights up. And everyone in the gym sees how you two always stare at each other."

I shrug off my sweater because it is suddenly warm. "Are you asking if Rey and I are together?"

He rubs the back of his neck, and he lets out a breath. "Maybe? No. Um... Are you?"

I clear my throat. "No. Rey and I aren't together. Like I said, he's my boss."

My phone dings, and I retrieve it from my side pocket.

Rey: What does he want?

Ari: Nothing, we are just talking. When I pulled in, he heard my car making an awful noise and offered to take a look.

Rey: Why is he still talking to you, Ari?

I look up, and Chase quirks a brow. "Is everything okay?"

My thumbs hover over the screen as I look at Chase, and I don't know if I should be angry. Does Rey think I'm flirting, or is he being overprotective?

Ari: Why can't he talk to me, Rey?

Rey: Is it about his membership at the gym? Is it gym related?

Ari: Not really.

Rey: Do I have to show you why?

"I think you should go," I tell Chase, trying to get him to leave before Rey shows up, but I'm too late. Rey is standing right behind him with a scowl on his face.

"Hey, champ," Chase says with a smile. Rey blinks.

Sometimes I forget that people don't know he's deaf. That he can't hear a word they're saying. People overlook his silence. They accept that it's in his nature. That he was built not to say a word. That he fought enough in his lifetime to have the privilege not to.

Chase lowers his gaze when Rey ignores him and motions for me to come to him with his hand.

"Is there something you need, Rey?" I say slowly so he can understand, trying to hide the truth, but it doesn't matter. Rey's impenetrable gaze sends a message you don't need to hear.

Chase felt it. I felt it. He wanted Chase to leave.

Chase glances at me. "I'll see you around, Ari," he says, looking back at Rey apologetically. "I hope I didn't get her in trouble."

Rey's eyes are like boiling chocolate when they glance at Chase, waiting for him to hurry out of the room.

Rey slams the door shut and closes the blinds. When he turns around, I expect him to be angry with me, but his face is unreadable.

"What are you doing?" I sign. "Why did you do that?"

"What did he really want?"

"Nothing."

He arches a sarcastic brow, then looks me up and down. "Nothing? Is that why he was worried he got you in trouble?"

He understood. But why is he acting like this? What did I do wrong?

"Is this about the rule?" He flashes his straight white teeth like a predator finally cornering his prey. "Do you think closing the door and closing the blinds helps?"

"Do you think I care what anyone out there thinks?" he signs.

I nod. "Yes, I do," I sign.

I want to remind him that he does, or he wouldn't have made the rule that day in the kitchen.

"You don't want me talking to the guys, but I can't treat them like shit every time they spark up a conversation with me."

"Why not?"

"Because it's rude. It's bad for business."

"The only business they have here is to train, not chat up the office girl." I flinch like he slapped me.

Of course, that's how he sees me. To him, I'm the office girl—incapable of handling the attention from a couple of male athletes, a distraction, and weak. Not strong enough to make it out alone, like a bird that needs shelter because it hasn't learned to fly since it was hurt. It's what everyone in my life thinks of me. My parents. Jimmy. His friends. And now Rey.

"Well, if you don't need anything work-related from me, I have work to do, and you have a gym to run." I grab a pen and the notepad, dismissing him.

He slams his hand on the table, causing me to jolt. He leans across the desk, his face inches from mine. The veins bulge from his forearms. His eyes burn with a heat that causes me to tremble.

"Let them think," he whispers, causing shivers to race down my neck, "that I have your face down on this desk." I catch a slight accent in his words that I find attractive. It makes my heart race.

"But you wouldn't," I say, staring at his lips. How close they are to mine. The scent of his sweat and cologne.

I imagine him taking me from behind. Would he be gentle or rough? My guess is by the way he is looking at me right now, he wouldn't.

He finally pulls away, leaving me staring at him as he walks out the door.

REY

I LOOK UP, knowing exactly what he's talking about.
I didn't like how he made her smile or how Chase looked at her.

He's right, but I don't want to admit it.

Rey: She needs a car. I don't think the one
she has now is worth fixing.

Javier: You have millions in the bank. Go
buy her one.

Rey: What if she won't take it?

Javier: Did you ask her?

Rey: It's complicated.

Javier: Let her go, Rey.

I pocket my phone and slide into the ring where Chase is
ready to train.

————

Scanning the kitchen after my Saturday morning run, I don't
see Ari. Javier walks in and heads directly toward his room, not
finding it weird that she isn't sitting at the breakfast table or
cooking up a storm.

Instead of heading to my room for a shower, I walk up the
stairs, telling myself it's to check if she is feeling alright. She's
been studying every day this past week. With Javier's fight
looming, I used the time to get him ready. Train him hard the
same way I train right before a fight.

But I can't shake the feeling that something isn't right. Like
the air has changed, Ari's strawberry smell has faded from the
house like a distant memory.

She has been upset with me ever since the incident with
Chase. I sent him a text to apologize. I didn't do it for him. I
did it for her.

I turn the knob of her bedroom, expecting to see her
propped on the bed studying with her book open, a notepad

on her lap, and a laptop open with the light from the screen shining on her gorgeous face, lost in thought, but the bed is empty.

Panic seizes my chest when I look around the room and find her stuff missing. I check the closet and en suite bathroom. I try to get air in my lungs, but all I can see are spots from breathing so hard.

I bolt down the stairs and scan the driveway, hoping that her Honda is parked like an eyesore, but that, too, is gone. She left. She left and didn't tell me.

I pull out my phone and text her, hoping she's okay. If she's cold or, worse, her car has given up and she's stranded on the side of the road. If she's safe or hungry.

My brother appears at the front door, and I know it's none of those things.

She's gone.

Rey: I'm sorry.

I STARE AT THE MESSAGE, not having the courage to delete it. I moved in three days ago but wanted to wait until the weekend when it was less busy. Since Javier's fight is tomorrow, I don't need to come to work on Saturday, so I moved my things before they returned from their morning run. Javier promised not to tell Rey before I left. I didn't know how to tell Rey about the apartment or see the look in his eyes when I did. It was better this way. He wouldn't have to feel guilty watching me leave.

The apartment feels lonely, and it's mostly empty, but it's mine. A place I can call my own. I won't feel like I'm a burden to anyone, and it's a fresh start—my fresh start.

Since it's a short walk to campus, I junked my car.

Two days ago, I took it to a mechanic, who said I was lucky it lasted this long. He said it was better to get something for it now than when it would cost me to tow it to a junkyard.

Uber wasn't so bad. Javier offered to bring me and pick me up, but I told him I would manage. He offered to pay for the rides for working at the gym, and I couldn't refute the offer, so I agreed.

I stare at Rey's text, not knowing what to say. I typed and retyped. Typed again.

Finally....

> Ari: Thank you for all you have done for me,
> Rey. Tell Javier good luck and to call me
> when he wins.

Three little bubbles pop up and then disappear.

Around midnight, Javier was declared the winner by TKO. The look on Javier's face from the picture on social media told me that I wouldn't be receiving a call from Javier.

He was doing fine, but it was going to be a long night of celebrating and recuperation. I felt a slight pang of hope in my chest, wishing that Rey would send me a text. However, I stopped checking my phone by three in the morning. Through tears, I kept reassuring myself that it was for the best.

———

When I hear a light knock, I look up and am surprised to see Chase in the office doorway. Javier told me that Rey apologized via text to Chase, but I didn't think he would talk to me after what happened.

"How are you?"

"I'm good, I guess. How is everything going with you?"

His smile brightens. "I'm good, actually. I'm going to start fighting professionally."

"Really?" I say with a bright smile. "That's great, Chase. Are you any good?" I tease.

"I don't know. You will have to see for yourself."

"Let me know when the fight is, and I'll be the judge."

"Okay. On one condition."

"What's that?"

"You go out with me to dinner."

I lift my long hair from the nape of my neck. "Wow," I say, fanning myself. "Is it hot in here?"

He laughs, and I notice he has dimples. "That depends."

"Depends on what?"

He walks closer. I automatically look out the tiny window, expecting to see Rey's gaze aimed at me like it always is, but he's not looking this way. He's hitting the bag with his headphones on.

Since the day I left his house, Rey hasn't looked at me the same way like a thousand suns burning into my soul. He hasn't texted me to ask if I'm alright. To see if I made it home after work.

After three weeks, Rey didn't think of me anymore. Not in the way I thought of him.

"If you're here."

I look up. "Huh?" He arches a brow. I blush, embarrassed that I wasn't paying attention.

"I said, if you are here, Ari."

I smile. "Oh."

He pushes off the wall and lowers his voice. "How about it? You and me hang out on a Friday night."

"I can't. Um... I don't have a car. My car died at the junkyard."

He pinches his brows. "How have you been getting to work?"

I pick up the pen and begin to click it open and closed, open and closed. "I take an Uber to and from my apartment."

"Late at night?" he asks, bewildered.

"Yep. The good news is that the gym pays for it. I don't think anyone would try anything if they picked me up from here. The Uber guy probably thinks I can kick his ass," I say with a laugh.

"Oh," he says confused. "That's great...free Uber rides."

"It was Javier's idea."

I could tell by his expression that he was surprised that Rey wasn't opposed to it after the gym closed, but he didn't say anything, and I was grateful.

In truth, I need a friend. I want to talk to someone who isn't part of Jimmy's circle. I was caught up in his life for so long that I didn't realize I was living alone. Every friend I had since I arrived at college was through Jimmy.

"Alright, Friday night. We can go see a late movie or maybe get something to eat you haven't tried."

"I would like that," I say while he pulls out his phone. "What's your number?"

I rattle off my number, and he sends me a text.

Chase: What time? We should text. I don't want you to get in trouble with your boss.

Ari: Very funny. But on a side note, I'm not allowed to fraternize with members of the gym.

He shrugs and gives me a wink. "You're not. We're friends."

"Ten," I whisper with a smile.

"Cancel the Uber. I'll make it back in time to take you home today. I'll wait in the parking lot until you're ready."

"Are you sure?"

"Uber drivers aren't all that safe."

There have been horror stories.

I look out the window when Chase leaves the office, but Rey is gone. He isn't near the punching bag or in the ring. It's like he vanished.

I'M WORKING on the bag, but I'm watching Ari collect her things in the office from my peripheral vision. I check my phone for the time, and it's five minutes to ten. I wait every night until she leaves. Making sure the Uber driver takes her home. I want nothing more than to be near her. To steal her breath. Smell her sweet skin. It takes everything inside me not to walk into the office and beg her to return. To not leave me.

When I get home, I look for her in the house sometimes. At times, I think she is still in her room. There are nights when I can't sleep thinking about her and walk to her room and lie on the bed, hoping the housekeeper hasn't forgotten to not wash the scent of her from the sheets. I sniff the bed like a dog, trying to find its owner's scent until I see it by the small pillows. I close my eyes, imagining her in my arms, and when I wake up alone, I'll find her in the kitchen making us food and wearing those sexy shorts I love, but I know it was just a dream. The ghost of her lives in my thoughts. Her heartbeat is the only sound I can remember.

My phone pings from a notification. I unlock the screen and frown. Her Uber ride has been canceled on my account.

I look up in time to see Ari turn off the lights. She doesn't look this way. She doesn't stare at me when I'm on the speed bag or find me when I'm in the ring. She only communicates with me through Javier. I hate it but have accepted it if that's what she wants.

I've stopped texting her and try to get used to her not being in my life, but I can't think. I can't breathe.

I miss her.

I grab my shirt, pull it over my head, and reach for my sweater as she walks toward the exit to tell her that her ride will not be waiting outside. I could have texted her, but it would have taken too long, and I didn't want her standing outside alone in the cold. She pushes the door and walks out before I can reach her.

I run toward the exit, catching the door before it slams shut. I shiver from the cold as it bites my skin.

I spot a late-model Mustang pulling up. She turns her face slightly when she opens the door. I see her smile. The driver's side door opens. My stomach clenches as I watch Chase walk around and help her in his car.

I swallow the thickness in my throat, stepping back inside and letting the door slam shut. I close my eyes, and all I can see is him kissing her. Making love to her.

Pain stabs me in the chest. It feels like the final round of a fight. Feeling every cut and bruise on my swollen face. Every breath I take burns like I'm on fire, and I can do nothing to make it stop unless I give up. It's too late, but I can't let her go.

I walk over to the punching bag, and rain blows until the bag splits.

I stop. I drop to my knees, gripping the bag to keep myself from falling. My lungs burn. Tears sting my eyes.

Strong arms wrap around me from behind. I whirl around, ready to strike, but it's Javier. My eyes blur, and I cry for the first time since my father left us. I cry, listening to the silence that is swallowing everything I love.

ARI

I HEAD INTO THE OFFICE, and my stomach drops when I see Rey inside, hanging Javier's belt next to his in the glass case. Rey must be proud of him. I can see it in his eyes when he looks at Javier with love and admiration.

When Rey finally notices me, he closes the glass, turns the lock, and steps to the side so I can get behind the desk.

He leans close when I walk past. It's not enough to touch me, but enough that I swear I could feel the intake of his breath like he was breathing me in.

His fingers lightly brush my hand, sending a signal to my heart.

I look up, and his eyes fixate on me like they hold a big secret.

I'm lost. Trapped in the power of his spell.

My heart screams at him to have mercy on me.

I sit in the chair and place my purse in the bottom drawer.

He doesn't move. I could never get tired of watching the hard lines of his face. The fullness of his mouth. Remembering how they felt when they pressed on my skin.

I pull out my phone. His eyes drop to the screen. Then, slowly, he moves to my face, watching me like he always does, causing my pulse to thump in my neck. The mystery that is Rey entangles me in its grip.

Hoping. Yearning.

Because I love him.

The seconds ticking by feel like years. I send Javier a message.

> Ari: I'm sorry to bother you, but Rey is in the office. He's been staring at me after putting your belt on the shelf beside his. It looks awesome, by the way. Could you ask him what he needs, and I will get right on it?

I never thought my relationship with Rey would come to this after everything, but it has. I can't torture myself. I can't love someone who doesn't want to love me in return.

Rey looks down at his phone when it goes off. He types in a response.

My phone dings from an incoming message before he walks out.

> Rey: I never thought my heart would break from hearing your silence.

I rush out of the office. His words break me apart like his fists right now, connecting with the bag like lightning when it strikes.

Everyone in the gym stops what they are doing. They watch, thinking he's training, but I know whatever he has deep inside is ripping him apart, keeping him from being happy. He deserves to be loved the way he deserves.

All I can think about is taking it away. Healing his pain. Telling him that there is no such thing as silence between us. It doesn't exist because I'm his.

———

"Thanks for the ride."

"Anytime, gorgeous."

He kisses me on the cheek before I shut the door.

Chase is a nice guy who makes sure I get home safely and walks me to my door.

I double-check the lock on my front door before I go to take a hot shower. I finished my homework on campus before heading to the gym. I look around my empty apartment. After sleeping in my car and gas station bathrooms, I'm proud to be able to support myself.

I finally called my parents and told them I had moved into an apartment on my own and found a job.

When I step out of the shower, the steam fogs up the vanity mirror, and my phone vibrates. I unlock it, hoping it's spam, but my stomach drops when I see it's from Javier. I hate the way Rey feels. I hate that I can't reach him emotionally, and I don't know what is going through his mind.

> Javier: Ari, I need your help. My brother sucks at making soup, and it's too late to order takeout. Can you come over and help a guy out?

I smile. Javier has been recovering from his fight. He had a swollen eye and jaw, but thankfully, he is okay and was cleared by the doctor to stay home with pain meds for six weeks. When he came home, he had bruises all over his body.

There is no way I can get an Uber to his house at this time of night.

> Ari: I'm already home, Javier. I don't have a car, and it's late.

> Javier: Please, Ari. I'm starving, and Rey
> sucks at cooking. The soup he made tastes
> like old salt water.

I giggle because it's true. Rey can't cook for shit. He made lunch for Javier and almost gagged. He let me taste the chicken, and it tasted like cardboard. It was horrible.

> Ari: I can't order an Uber now. How am I
> going to get to school in the morning? I
> have a class.

> Rey: Open the door, Ari.

I jolt when I hear a knock on my front door. My heart starts racing. My knees shake.

> Javier: Rey should be there to pick you up
> soon. You can take my truck if you want. I
> don't care. I need you, Ari. Please.

With a sigh, I practically drag my feet across the carpet to the front door and unlock it.

The door swings open, and I shiver as a rush of frigid air assaults my face and hair.

Rey walks right in, causing me to step back. He shuts the door behind him, his broad frame like a wall.

His eyes roam the interior space of the apartment. There isn't much to see except that it's clean with no furniture.

"You're here to pick me up because you can't cook soup?" I sign.

He nods, giving me a shrug.

"I need to dry my—" I point at my wet hair. He nods.

I walk into my bedroom to blow-dry my hair in front of

the vanity mirror. I'm picking up the blow-dryer when I feel a tap on my shoulder.

I turn around, and his lips form a thin line. I place the dryer and brush with a thud on the vanity counter.

"What's wrong?" I sign.

He points at the inflatable bed with the cute little pillows I bought from Walmart and then looks at me grimly.

I raise my chin. "I don't have money for a bed," I sign, pointing at the inflatable mattress. "That... is what I can afford." I shrug my shoulders. "It's not that bad once you get used to it."

He shakes his head disapprovingly. I turn around to dry my hair. He leans on the wall with his jaw set and arms firmly crossed over his massive chest.

Obviously, he has a problem with my sleeping arrangements, but this is my life until I can find a job that pays me more.

I watch him pull at the neck of his hoodie. It must be getting warm from the blow-dryer's heat. I turn around and place the round brush on the counter. He hands me my phone.

He pulls his hoodie off with one hand, his bicep bulging as he does it. Why is that so damn sexy?

My eyes trail over his ab muscles when his shirt rises. My phone goes off. I look at the screen.

> Rey: I'm ashamed that you sleep uncomfortably. That you don't have a bed when you could have mine.

I place my phone on the vanity and turn on the blow-dryer. I can't do this with him.

After I finish drying my hair, I make my way to the closet. I take out a set of thermal leggings, an oversized cream sweater, and UGG-styled shoes.

I'm about to remove my robe when he hasn't left my room. In fact, he's leaning against the doorjamb, arms crossed, staring at me with fire in his eyes. I nudge my head, telling him to go wait out in the living room, but he doesn't budge. I place my hands on my hips.

"Really?" I mouth.

He licks his lips. Heat pulses between my thighs. He watches. He waits. His intense stare and the sight of his physique traps me in his bubble. A bubble where nothing matters but us. Nothing can come in, and nothing can go out. No words are needed; it is just the energy surrounding us now.

I'm irrevocably in love with him.

In my mind, he is part of me. I can take back the piece of my heart and place it inside me, but it doesn't matter because he is imprinted. Rey is imprinted in my mind, heart, and in my soul.

He walks closer until he is inches from me. His eyes burn with desire. He touches my face with two fingers, leaving goose bumps in his wake. I briefly close my eyes, and just for a minute, I let myself... feel.

He leans close and touches his lips to my forehead, causing the scent of him to swirl around me. I inhale him deeply, memorizing his scent again, just for a second, until he pulls away.

"I-I miss you, Ari," he stammers. His voice is struggling with emotion.

I open my eyes but don't look at him. I grab my clothes and walk to the bathroom to change.

Once I close the door, I lean back and let the emotion that has been building behind my eyes go. Tears begin to scar my cheeks like hot lava dripping down my chin. I sniff after a sob leaves my chest and wipe my eyes.

"Get a grip, Ari," I mutter to myself. I look at my reflection and turn on the faucet to wash my face so he won't know I was crying. I quickly dress and with one last look in the mirror, let out a deep breath and open the door.

I leave the bathroom, and he waits for me in the living room. I grab my bag, phone, and keys. He walks over to me and lifts my chin to look into my eyes. His expression tells me that he's noticed I was crying, and he isn't happy, but he signs, "Why are you crying?"

"I wasn't crying," I sign in response. "You're right. You are a terrible liar."

After we are both outside, he opens the door, and I lock it. He leads the way to the parking lot, but I don't see his Range Rover. He lightly touches my elbow and leads me to a white SUV with red seats that look brand new.

I point at the car questioningly. It's a Mercedes SUV that looks like a Jeep, and it's gorgeous. He smiles and holds out the key. He moves to the driver's side and opens the door but steps back, waiting for me to enter.

I look at him with a confused expression and sign, "You want me to drive?"

He nods approvingly. "Okay," I sign.

He makes sure the driver's seat is adjusted to my height. The interior is beautiful, and the light glow inside the cabin is pretty. It reminds me of the sensory lights he has in his home.

The way it drives is amazing. I look at all the lights on the dash with the fancy screen. The car smells like heaven. It will probably take me a month to figure out how to use all the features.

After the twenty-minute drive, he pushes the garage door opener, and his gate opens. I drive the car down his driveway and notice he doesn't open the garage. I brake, and he points at the nearest spot by the entrance. I place the vehicle in park and rub my hand over the Mercedes symbol on the steering wheel, loving the feel of it under my fingers.

"It's beautiful," I sign.

He pulls out an envelope with papers tucked inside the glove compartment, takes the keyless fob, and hands it to me. I look up in confusion. He takes his phone and sends me a message before I can read what is inside the envelope.

> Rey: I'm glad you like it, Ari. I hope you don't mind, but it's my gift. I ordered it two weeks ago, and it was delivered today. I'm sorry you had to take so many Ubers, but the car I bought for you had to be perfect, and I'm glad I was right.

My eyes fill with tears, and my throat gets thick with emotion. No one has ever given me something so beautiful. This car must have cost him a fortune.

> Ari: I don't know what to say, Rey.

I look up, and my eyes are full of unshed tears. He grins and tilts his head toward his phone.

> Rey: You deserve it, Ari. If it weren't for you, I wouldn't have been able to manage the boxing gym and train Javier and the other fighters. I also got this for you because you mean the world to me. I know I might be too late, but I wanted you to know.

> Ari: Thank you, Rey. I love it.

Javier turns his head on the three stacked pillows under

him and grimaces at the sudden movement. He is still sore. He thought he could return to training, but it was too soon.

"Hey," I say, greeting him. "You can stop pretending."

He raises his hands in the air like he's in prayer. "Thank God. My favorite woman on the planet is here. How do you like your new car, princess?"

My cheeks burn hot, and Rey passes by me with a smile on his lips, taking my bag upstairs. "I love it! Who wouldn't? It's gorgeous."

"I see he gave you the papers. He placed it in your name and took care of all the details. He has been driving me crazy getting you that car. He had the dealership special order it for you. I'm sorry you had to take Ubers for so long, but we knew you wouldn't borrow any of his other cars."

"He told me, but he didn't have to do that, Javier."

He waves his arm. "I think he has the Ari bug, so watch out. He might sting," he says, wiggling his eyebrows.

I laugh. "You're crazy."

He points at Rey coming down the stairs. "You need to teach him how to cook, Ari. He sucks."

"I'm going to start your soup."

He nods with a content smile on his face. "Thank God you're back."

ARI

AFTER MAKING Javier his soup and cleaning up the kitchen, I go upstairs. The door to the room I used to stay in is open, and I notice that my things are not there.

I walk toward Rey's room and push the button for the light, which means someone is knocking on the door. I don't want to barge in. He might not be dressed, not that I would mind seeing him naked again. I shut my eyes tight and think of unicorns. I'm hoping it will work, but when he opens the door, he is shirtless, and unicorns become the furthest thing from my mind.

He's in nothing except his boxers. I unconsciously bite my lip because what is a girl to do when the man she loves is standing in front of her barely dressed?

His ab muscles ripple like they want my hands. The trail of the deep V disappearing down like two valleys into the band of his boxers causes saliva to pool in my mouth.

He has a body that you wouldn't mind working on your house or, better yet, in your house. If it meant having him over to fix and leave, I would purposely put holes in all my pipes just to watch him come over.

He steps aside, and I walk in.

Lights are on, casting a blue glow around the room, and I notice he placed my bag near his closet.

I point at my bag and give him a questioning look. He points at his bed, and I shake my head.

He wants me to sleep in his room. He pulls me by the hand inside, pushing the door close.

"I want to... hold you," he rasps. "I'm sorry if...I hurt you."

I shake my head again. I close my eyes and count backward from ten to zero.

"Please, Ari?" he says in a hoarse voice.

He speaks to me more and more, and I know, deep down, he's doing it for me. He wants me to see him, and I want to tell him that I already do. I can see his beautiful soul underneath the anger.

There's a hidden emotion in his eyes when he looks at me. I wrap my arms around him. Standing on my toes, I pull him toward me, embracing his warmth. Not wanting to ever let him go.

He walks me back, and we fall on the mattress. The soft comforter is like a soft pillow on my back.

I give him a sultry smile. His eyes never leave mine. His mouth parts. He looks down between us. He swallows thickly and says, "You're...beautiful. *Preciosa.*"

"When was the last time you spoke?" I sign. "Before me."

He straddles me and signs, "Thirteen. When my father left and never came back. He left because he didn't want to raise a deaf son."

Tears fill my eyes, but I blink them away.

I touch his neck and lean down to suck each spot gently, and with every place my lips feel, I place a tender kiss like taking pieces of the different flavors belonging to him in my mouth. His hands slide down my waist, and I arch against him, wanting to take all his hurt and pain.

He groans when my hands land on his pecs, and I caress his chest slowly down to his abs. He pushes my hands, pinning them hard over my head with his hand. His nostrils flare, and I can tell he is trying to control himself when I feel his hard erection pressing roughly between my legs.

I can feel him shake, his other hand gripping my thigh. He holds me tight in this position. I should be scared, but I wasn't because I knew the tenderness he hid underneath. He thinks he isn't good enough to deserve love because the person he loved and admired growing up abandoned him.

I could never abandon him if he wanted me. If he chose me.

He releases my hands. I caress the side of his cheek and his jaw and say slowly, "Your voice is beautiful."

His lips find mine, and we kiss while his hand pulls my leggings and underwear down my thighs. He pushes my shirt over my ribs, marking my skin with his fingers. He dips his head, licking the marks with his tongue. He finds my bare breasts. He sucks and grazes my nipples with his teeth. My arms lift, and he removes my shirt, and I'm completely naked.

I feel fragile like a small flower under his gaze as he devours my body with his eyes. I writhe and tremble. He's real. His body is hard and sculpted. A landscaper of hard lines and edges. Raw power capable of destroying anything in his path, but he holds me by my thighs with his face between my legs.

He's the first man who's ever wanted me this way. The first man to pleasure me with his mouth.

I don't know what to do with my hands when my thighs tremble. I place them on my chest like it's my first time having sex.

He knew I wasn't a virgin, but I had only ever been with Jimmy, and it wasn't special. It was fast, and there were times I never finished. Many times.

He looks up, and I could tell he knows. He knows I have never been kissed there. He pinches his brows like he is absorbing it. Like he is piecing the things I told him together. When he found me, I was lost like a boat adrift at sea. I surrendered to him, giving him my love and soul in the chaos of newfound love. He positions his mouth over me. I caress his cheek when he flicks his tongue, igniting every nerve ending I possess. I moan, gripping his hair and pulling at his dark strands as he devours me. I arch my back, watching the lights in his room cast shadows over the ceiling in a kaleidoscope of colors. His tongue licks every inch of me, robbing me of my breath, my voice, and my heart. I am his. Irrevocably his.

Stars explode behind my eyes when I come. I'm incapable of speaking when he looks up, his mouth wet with the taste of me on his lips.

I quiver.

"Don't look...away from me," he says with a tremor in his voice, emotion burning in his eyes.

He holds himself above me. I touch his neck and lean down to suck each spot gently, and with every place my lips feel, I place a tender kiss like taking pieces of the different flavors belonging to him in my mouth. His hands slide down my waist, and I arch against him. He groans when my hands land on his pecs, and I caress his chest slowly down to his abs.

I trace his tattoos with my tongue, loving the feel of him under my hands. The strong muscles of his shoulders. The tip of his cock is between my thighs. He looks up for a moment, holding my gaze. My heart beat for him to take me. There was nothing between us.

His eyes slide to where my thighs are spread open, then back up to my eyes. He grips my face gently with one hand. His lips are a breath away as he enters me, hard and deep. I grip his hips, and my fingers slide over the hard muscle of his ass when he pushes into me the rest of the way. His eyes bore into mine, holding me in his gaze.

I could see the boy he was, yearning for love. Lost and alone. Losing the love he adored, seeking to be accepted as a man with all his flaws, and fearful of being abandoned. Now a man. Gorgeous and lethal. One hand clutches my ribs, the other still holding my face gently as he makes love to me, riding me like a storm with crashing waves.

He rests his forehead against mine. "Ari," he whispers, placing both palms flat against the mattress above me when he feels me tremble right before I come like a lightning strike.

"Rey," I moan breathlessly against his lips.

His body shakes when his hips grind into me faster and harder, matching his breaths. He comes, taking my lips with his teeth, robbing me of breath and spilling inside me.

I lean forward and slide my tongue in his mouth while he reaches with his hand over my neck, placing his thumb to feel my pulse beating. He smiles against my lips.

We feel perfect together, our bodies coming alive like a living, breathing being inside us.

REY

I GO on my morning run, but when I come back, Ari has already left. I didn't have bad dreams about her leaving me this time. She stayed the night and fell asleep in my arms.

She's everything. She's perfect. I don't care if I sound funny or if I'm too loud when I talk. I've been practicing every day in front of the mirror.

Whatever I want to say, I want her to hear it.

I want her to know how much I love her. I tried to tell her, but I feared it was too soon.

"Have fun last night?" Javier signs with a playful smirk.

I give him the finger and then sign, "What's wrong? Jealous?"

"Of you? With a girl like Ari? Hell, yes," he admits. "I mean no disrespect, but she is hot. When she wears shorts or leggings..." He grimaces in pain and then smiles. "You had sex with her last night," he signs.

I look away because he knows I don't like talking about Ari like that.

"Are you ever going to speak to me?" I look directly at him. I know it bothers him that I gave her something I took away from my brother and mother. Not even the psychologist understood why I refused a hearing aid and lost my ability to speak. "You can, you know. I didn't tell Mom. I thought it was best if it came from you, but I know you have been trying because of Ari. It's okay to admit you love her, Rey. She won't leave you if you tell her. If there is anyone I'm sure of that could love you, it would be her."

I change the subject. I'm not ready to talk about my feelings or what to do.

I tell Javier about Ari's lack of furniture in her apartment and how we are underpaying her. We agree on how much I want to pay her, not taking it out of his share but strictly from my own.

I spend the afternoon thinking about her. The way she looked at me after I made love to her. It was her I had eyes for. Her skin I smelled. The words I practiced were for her. Like a gift I wanted no one else to have.

> Rey: Hi, beautiful. Let me know when you get out of class and are heading out. I want to make sure you are okay. I miss you, Ari.

> Ari: I will be heading out in ten. I'll see you very soon. Miss you, too, Rey.

I smile and begin to plan for a special night. A night she will remember.

I park my Range Rover, walk into the gym, and check my phone like a crazy person to see if she's texted me back.

After an hour, I feel my phone vibrate while hitting the punching bag. I calm my breathing, hold the punching bag, and retrieve my phone.

> Ari: I'm pulling in, but I will warn you that a flower courier is outside. Jimmy doesn't get that I don't want to be with him, and he won't stop texting me. I don't want to bother you with my problems, but I don't want you to think the worst.

Rey: Ari, you don't have to explain
anything. If he's bothering you, tell me. I'll
handle it.

Ari: I don't want to make a big deal about
it. I figured he would have gotten the hint.

Like she said, the flower courier arrives, and I walk over. The delivery guy pulls out a paper, and before he moves his lips, I grab the bouquet of roses and toss them in the trash. I pick up the card that floated to the floor with her name scrolled over it. I give him a hard glare that has him backing away with his hands in the air.

I open it, and it reads.

Ari,

I love you, and I miss you. I'm not going to give up until you come home.

Love you, Jimmy

I don't like his behavior. This guy can't accept that she wants nothing to do with him and has moved on.

Ari is mine, and I protect what is mine. I place my headphones over my ears and turn up the volume to the highest level.

As usual, I take my frustration out on the bag until Ari walks in.

I picture Jimmy's face, and I hit the bag more forcefully. I hit it repeatedly in multiple combinations, and it's like I'm fighting for my title, except this time, the prize is Ari's heart.

ARI

I PLACE my cell phone down in frustration. This is Jimmy's third message today, and I don't know how many since the flower delivery yesterday.

It has been hell since last week.

I had to cut my time with Chase short on Friday because of testing, Jimmy, and my thoughts about Rey. He was nice, and like me, he needed a friend.

Chase just ended a two-year relationship and wants to find himself. We went to eat at a nice restaurant and talked about past relationships. I brought up what I went through with Jimmy and even spoke about Rey.

I left out the part about him being deaf and just kept it that Rey is a quiet guy because, in all reality, Rey is quiet by nature. He keeps things bottled up.

No, he needs a maid to help him clean and baby him. He

treated me like his slave. I cooked, cleaned, and drove him around so he would have enough time to screw around.

The first thing I did before calling the housing office on campus was to get tested for everything at the clinic. I was relieved I was clean, but it was scary. I have always been on birth control since my first time with Jimmy and was always careful not to get pregnant.

As a fighter, Rey gets tested often, and I know he does because there was a medical file on both Javier and Rey in the mess in his office. The last one was right before Javier's fight in Vegas.

I didn't need to ask if Rey was clean because I knew he was.

Rey has this way of making me feel comfortable. I didn't have that with Jimmy, but I didn't realize it until I was around Rey.

The gym has seen increased sign-ups since Javier's last fight, which has made The Sweat Box a success. When I pull up, the parking lot is full, even on a Thursday, when it was our slowest day.

Other fighters from our gym have also been improving and winning in different weight classes.

I'm proud of Rey and what he has accomplished. He struggled and came from nothing.

After his father left, he sacrificed not going to college to fight for a dream and make enough money to support his brother and mother.

I jolt when I hear, "Nice car."

Jimmy leans on his sports car, watching me walk toward the gym entrance. I didn't notice his Porsche since it's low compared to my SUV.

I lock my car. "Leave me alone, Jimmy."

"I can't do that, Ari," he interjects.

Fear crawls down my spine. I grip my bag tighter on my shoulder, and my hands sweat despite the cold weather.

"You can, and you will. It's over. I told you this."

He points his finger at my car. "I can treat you just as nice, Ari. I can buy you nice things."

"I don't want you to buy me anything. I want you to leave me alone," I demand.

I slide my hand into my pocket to get my phone. I play it off because Jimmy is desperate. He doesn't look like himself. He looks like a lion about to pounce on the gazelle—me being the gazelle.

I move toward the entrance, and he blocks my path. I narrow my gaze at him and notice he hasn't slept. He has dark circles under his eyes. He looks haggard and disheveled. "I need to get into work."

"You can be a couple of minutes late. Your boss won't mind. I know you're fucking him. I didn't think you were down like that, but you've been full of surprises lately."

I grind my teeth, and I feel like they are about to snap. "I think you better leave. Stop following me, stop texting, and stop sending me flowers. I. Don't. Want. You."

His fists clench. "I love you, and he doesn't! I can't stop thinking about you fucking him. Working with him while he looks at you. You're such a hypocrite, Ari." He points at his chest. "I was your first. I was the one who took care of you so you didn't have to sleep in the dorms and take on more debt. Me."

"I didn't ask you to do any of that. You begged me to move in with you, which was my biggest mistake. You treated me like I was your glorified housekeeper and personal driver. You shoved me, and I fell. Instead of seeing if I was okay, you threatened me. I'm sorry, but if that is how you love, then I think I'll pass."

I move, sidestepping him to make it to the door of the gym. I'm relieved when I get inside and walk down the hallway that leads to the office.

I hear the door open behind me. Everything happens so fast. I see a hand flash by my head, gripping my hair hard. Pain explodes over my skull as he tugs me backward.

"We weren't done talking, Ari." I gasp and drop my bag on the floor. I grip his hand with my fingers, trying to free it from my hair, but it's tight, and Jimmy is strong from playing hockey.

Tears pool in my eyes from the throbbing pain. "You're hurting me! Let go, Jimmy," I scream.

My instinct is to hit him, so I swing. I land a slap to his cheek, causing him to release me.

"You bitch!" he roars, lunging after me, but a big brick wall blocks Jimmy from reaching me.

I step back. Rey pushes Jimmy to the ground. A couple of guys from the gym rush over.

"Hey, man. You need to leave," one of the guys says. "Are you okay, Ari?" Ben asks, giving Jimmy a hard glare. "What the fuck, Jimmy?"

"What...you going to beat me up, Ben?"

Ben shakes his head, then his eyes lift to Rey's murderous glare. His chest heaves, full of rage. "But he is definitely going to fuck you up if you don't walk out of here, Jimmy. You put your hands on her. We all saw what you did. You crossed the line when you touched her."

Jimmy snarls at Rey. "Her pussy is good, isn't it?" he taunts.

I flinch at how vile and disrespectful Jimmy can be. I was naive and feel stupid for not seeing him for what he truly is—a glorified scumbag.

Jimmy sucks air through his teeth. He thinks Rey is

backing down, but I know better. Rey can't hear him because if he did, I'm sure Jimmy would be on the ground picking up his teeth off the floor.

I place my hand on Rey's arm, and he turns his head, but it is a mistake on my part because Jimmy takes the opportunity to punch Rey in the jaw.

"No, Jimmy!" I scream.

I look up at Rey, who staggers from the blow but shakes it off. His mouth is full of blood when he smiles at Jimmy, and then all bets are off.

Jimmy thinks he has the upper hand and lunges toward Rey, but Rey is faster and more skilled, and he bobs and weaves when Jimmy tries to land a punch.

All the other fighters crowd around to watch.

"Kick his ass, champ," one teenager says, watching how Rey dodges Jimmy's punches.

"Asshole deserves to be knocked the fuck out!" another guy shouts from the back.

"Stop it, Jimmy. Leave. You're going to get hurt," I warn him.

He snorts. "Please. I can take this pussy. He bleeds like everyone else."

The look in Rey's eyes is lethal. He could kill him with just one punch if he really wanted to. I'm terrified. This isn't a fight to Rey. This is war.

I wince when Rey swings, connecting with Jimmy's face. He splits his brow open, but knowing Jimmy, he won't back down. His pride won't allow it. Blood begins to drip down his face, but he keeps stepping forward, and at this point, there is nothing I can do.

Rey watches him closely. Jimmy spits on the floor. "Fuck you, how can you call yourself undefeated. I'm still standing."

"Jimmy, don't..."

Jimmy shakes his head. "Nope. Not until you come home. The only dick you'll be riding is mine."

Rey steps forward and hits him with a combination of punches, knocking Jimmy out cold on the ground.

I place my hands over my mouth to see how quickly Rey did it.

Rey stands over him and checks for a pulse. He nods that he is still alive. He must have read his lips, or maybe it was because Jimmy pulled my hair like he was ripping it from my skull.

I touch the part in my head and wince from the pain.

Asshole.

Rey walks over to me and lifts my chin. He takes a deep breath and looks down at me with a tenderness. He pinches his brows and grimaces when he notices that my head hurts.

He caresses my cheek with two fingers. "I will never..." He takes a deep breath. "Let anyone hurt you, Ari. I'm sorry... I was too late." A single tear rolls down his cheek, and my heart breaks wide open.

He looks up and sniffs, trying to rein in his emotions. "I l-love... you, Ari," he says off pitch.

Everyone stares in shock, waiting for me to respond, but I can't sign the words. I can't say them because he can't hear.

He closes his eyes in frustration and walks toward the locker room. I don't want him to just read it on my lips. I want it to be... more.

"Ben. Call the police and tell them what happened," I tell him.

"On it, Ari."

"Thanks. You might have to talk to the police. I don't want any of this coming back on Rey."

"We got it," Ben assures me. He nudges his chin toward the locker room. "Go take care of him."

I nod and run after Rey when he disappears into the locker room.

When I make sure the coast is clear and no one is inside, I enter to see where he went.

When I turn the corner by the lockers, I spot him sitting on one of the benches with his head bowed. I move to stand in front of him and motion for him to look up at me. His head lifts, and his face turns into a grimace when he licks the corner of his mouth, which has a slight cut and is already swelling.

I step back and sign, "I love you, too. Thank you for defending me. He could have hurt me if it weren't for you." I hold the sides of his face and look at him. "I. Love. You," I say slowly.

He smiles and makes an invisible cross with his hands over his chest.

"I prayed to God every night since you left my bed for you to love me," he signs. "I'm sorry I can't be like Noah. I can't build you a house, and I'm shit at writing love notes. They're almost as bad as my cooking. I've tried, Ari."

I smile and laugh as I sign, "I don't need a Noah. I need you, Rey."

"I'm better looking, and I have more money."

I shake my head and laugh. "Cocky much?" I sign.

He nods, and I lift his chin so I can inspect the damage. It isn't too bad, but he needs to put ice on it. It's already swelling.

After the police came and we gave our statements, they arrested Jimmy for assault and trespassing, and since Rey was defending me and did not throw the first punch, he wasn't charged.

I have to go to the police station and file a restraining order, but Rey sent a text to his lawyer and will go with me.

REY

I TOLD her I loved her in front of everyone in the gym. I know I must have sounded off tone or off pitch, but I don't care. She needed to know how I felt about her. When I saw Jimmy put his hands on her, I saw red. Something flashed before my eyes, imagining her hurt or, worse, him killing her. He was obsessed with getting her back. Guys like that are dangerous.

He won't bother Ari anymore, or I'll sue him and make sure the Flyers drops him. I'm angry with myself for not getting to her sooner. He could have hurt her. He wasn't in his right state of mind.

I'm still not convinced that he will leave her alone. I cannot let her out of my sight.

Something inside me just snapped like a dam of emotions, flooding me. I couldn't lose her. Never again. I will never allow it.

ARI

THE NEXT DAY, my head is sore from where Jimmy yanked me by my hair. I get up and get ready for class.

When I slide into the luxury SUV, I smile when I push the button, and it turns on.

It doesn't make a sound like my piece of crap Honda.

This baby purrs.

Before I place the car in reverse, my phone vibrates, and I look at the text.

> Rey: Don't back up. I'm right behind you.

I check the rearview mirror, and Rey's Range Rover is blocking me.

I smile and fire back a text.

> Ari: What are you doing here? I have to get to class.

> Rey: I'm here to drive you to class. Come get inside my car. It's warm.

I smile, shut off my car, get out, lock it up, and walk over to his.

When I'm inside, it is warm, but it also smells like Rey. I don't think I could get enough of his smell.

He opens his hand, and there are two pills, and he has a bottle of water in the other. He motions for me to take them, and I mutter, "Thank God."

I swallow down the pills with the water and text him.

> Ari: Thank you. My head feels like it got hit by a hammer.

> Rey: I figured that asshole pulled your beautiful hair, and you would feel worse in the morning. I'm sorry for showing up. A restraining order means if the cops are called, he will go to jail if he is caught or there is evidence that he is still contacting you or within five hundred feet of you, but it doesn't mean he won't try again.

> Ari: Thank you, Rey, for being there for me when he attacked me. I didn't realize how dangerous he was.

> Rey: He needs mental help, but I'm not taking any chances. What about breakfast?

> Ari: Yes, please.

He smiles and drives us to a breakfast café off campus. I feel warm in my jacket, leggings, and Uggs. It isn't snowing, but it is getting colder.

I think about what he said about mental health, and my thoughts go to his medical bill.

He parks out front.

> Ari: Why do you see a psychiatrist?

It takes him a second to respond. I watch something cross his features.

> Rey: I suffer from abandonment and have attachment issues. I have seen a psychiatrist since I lost my ability to hear. I was angry when kids would make fun of me. I stopped speaking. I refused a hearing aid.

Ari: Would it help you hear?

> Rey: Not in boxing. I couldn't wear it in the ring. I'm considered a deaf-mute, but the world doesn't know that.

Ari: I think you're amazing.

He glances at me, takes a deep breath, and slowly says, "I love you."

"I love you, too," I sign.

Some of the students recognize him. They smile. Some take pictures. I understand why he likes to go to small restaurants and diners.

I hope taking me out to breakfast doesn't make him uncomfortable.

We enter the café, and I look up at the menu waiting in line. I text him to ask what he would like.

He places a tender kiss on the top of my head.

> Rey: Coffee.

Ari: How do you like it?

> Rey: If you were in my bed this morning, you would know I like it with lots of cream and sugar.

I almost choke on my spit. The girl at the register looks at me with concern when I begin to cough. She looks at Rey and then at me. I raise a finger, telling her to give me a moment.

Then I hear Rey say loud enough, with a slight accent, "She needs a minute."

I start to laugh nervously when she says, "That's okay. It happens."

I finally place our order. I pull out my card when she rings us up, but he beats me to it and hands her his. I shake my head, and he nods. I roll my eyes playfully and step aside to the pickup line.

Rey drops me off, but not before giving me a scorching kiss on the lips. I lean into him, breathing in his scent, and sign, "I love you, Rey."

Instead of signing, he says, "I love you, Ari."

My heart melts—like ice under the sun. His voice is beautiful. He smiles and says, pacing himself, "I'll pick you... up at three."

I nod and blow him a kiss.

Walking toward the building, I notice his car doesn't drive off. He stays until he sees me safely inside.

When my classes for the day are over, the campus is buzzing with students. The sky is the color of metal. The wind blows the leaves, dragging them across the blades of grass.

As promised, Rey's Range Rover waits for me, but as I approach, he steps out of his car, and my heart skips a beat.

People were watching him walk around. He is a hulk of a man in his black hoodie. Tall, gorgeous, mysterious, and quiet.

"Do guys still do that?" a girl says, standing with a group of friends as Rey waits for me with the passenger door open. I want to jump into his arms, wrap my legs around him, and kiss his lips.

"He's so hot," the girl next to her says.

I never had a man wait for me and look at me the way Rey does.

Sometimes when you think you experience heartbreak, you

need to release it into the past so that true love can find you and start a new beginning.

REV

IT'S the second week that I've taken her to school, and I want to make sure she is safe. I know I'm being overprotective, but I can't take any chances.

I wait until she is in the office before working with the guys.

I'm getting to know some new faces. I will train them after Javier and my personal team teach them the basic skills and some more advanced skills.

I don't say much for obvious reasons, but I hate the twenty questions they throw at me when they think I can hear but act like I'm ignoring them. It's getting harder to deal with when I interact with people every day.

I catch some of the new guys glancing occasionally toward the office. I grind my teeth, trying to hide my anger. I get that Aria is attractive. She's beautiful.

I'm okay with an appreciative glance here and there.

Most of the older guys have gotten to know Ari, and they value her help. She organizes everything in the office and on the floor. Everything is clean and where it needs to be.

I'm showing one of the more seasoned fighters how to southpaw when I notice they are distracted.

I stop and snap my fingers to get their attention. They look over at me, and I widen my eyes.

I see one gesture with his thumb toward Ari from the

corner of my eye. Ben walks up and motions his hand over his neck, shaking his head disapprovingly at the guy.

Javier gives me a side glance and then glances at Ari. She is oblivious to what is happening, concentrating on getting the dirty towels in the washing machine and transferring the ones already washed to the dryer. Her leggings fit like a glove over her legs and perky ass. The Sweat Box T-shirt falls off her shoulder. Her hair is in two braids, and she looks good enough to eat.

> Javier: I suggest you do something about the guys regarding Ari. Now I understand what you meant about the rule of not bringing chicks to the gym. But this is Ari, Rey. She ignores them. She doesn't look this way, but you need to do something.

> Rey: What did this asshole in the ring say to you.

I watch Javier briefly close his eyes before he sends me a text.

> Javier: He said he was going to ask Ari out. I told him she had a boyfriend, but he said she wasn't married.

I look up and give him a smile. Anger brimming to the surface.

> Rey: I have to make a point.

Javier looks up from his phone and raises his eyebrows. I call out, "Ari!"

Her head snaps up, and she looks over at me, and I curl my finger for her to come over. The guys stop talking when she walks over with her cute little braids to the edge of the boxing ring.

She gives me a small smile, and I hold my hand to pull her up.

I ignore the knowing looks the guys give her.

I pull her against me and slide my hands to her waist. She smiles.

I bend and rub my nose against hers. She cups my face, and I lift her so she can wrap her legs around my waist.

Her eyes are locked on mine, and she passionately kisses my lips.

"I love you," I tell her, not caring if I sound weird, and watch her face blush.

"I love you, too," she responds sweetly with her lips.

I turn her around so her back is against my front and help her down from the ring.

When I turn around, all the guys look everywhere but at me. "She's mine," I growl.

The fighter I was teaching holds up his hands in mock surrender. I remember his name now. It's Marco. He says something, and I think it was my bad or sorry.

I don't want your apology, Marco. I want everyone to understand that Ari is mine.

She isn't off-limits. She is mine, and what is mine doesn't belong to anyone else.

It's not her fault. She doesn't do anything to attract attention on purpose because all her attention is on her job, school, and hopefully me.

ARI

AFTER TWO WEEKS of Rey picking me up and taking me to class, I pack an overnight bag and drive to his house. It is Friday night, and I don't have any homework or tests coming up. I thought I might surprise Rey. I don't think he would mind.

I get in my SUV and head toward his house. I'm excited to see Rey. I reach the gate of his home and press the garage door opener he programmed into the car.

I watch the gate open and drive through.

When the car crawls slowly down the driveway, I frown because a car is parked in front.

The door finally opens, and my heart drops. Julia.

What is she doing here?

She gives me a terribly fake smile. "Oh, hey, Ari. I was just out with Rey. He didn't mention that you would be stopping by."

My stomach clenches. I take a deep breath through my nose, forcing the knot down my throat.

"Is Rey here?" I ask a little too forcefully.

"I'm afraid he is in the shower," she says satisfactorily. "I came out to get the door since Javier went out tonight. I saw the lights go off— I really hate those lights. They can be distracting."

I take a step back like she slapped me. His bedroom? Is he

in the shower? I take a good look at her, and I notice that her hair is wet.

"You were in there with him?" I ask her.

"Yeah," she says, and shivers like her words didn't crush me. "I have to get back. It's cold out here."

"Of course," I tell her when she moves to close the door, trying to make sense of everything.

"Ari," she calls out.

I look over my shoulder with tears in my eyes. "Look, I've known Rey for a very long time, and he's an amazing guy but afraid of commitment. He always comes back to me. We've been doing this for years."

"Oh, you both deserve each other," I say scathingly.

I turn and walk away with my lip trembling. One tear falls, then another, and another.

I get in my car and drive for hours. Light blue streaks appear in the sky as the night fades. A couple of hours before daybreak, I park in front of my parents' driveway.

All night, my mind went numb, and I subconsciously remembered what day it was.

I practically run up the steps to the three-bedroom home I grew up in and close my eyes in relief that my key still works when it slides into the lock.

I hurry up the stairs to my room, not wanting to wake my parents. I tiptoe down the hallway and open my bedroom door. It looks the same. Just how I left it. The walls still have my favorite posters. Over the modest twin bed is the same comforter I had before I left for college.

I lift the pink sheets, slide into the bed, and turn off my phone.

I don't want to read what he has to say.

It was enough that my heart was breaking, scratching, and tearing me inside until nothing was left.

No one could take his place in my heart. He was part of me. The story I wanted to write. There was no future without him in it. No love deep enough. No words anyone could tell me that were more beautiful than the ones he spilled from his lips.

He didn't have to lie. He didn't have to tell me he loved me if he didn't feel it. I thought what we had was stronger than anything.

Stronger than words.

I don't want to believe her, but how do you explain her presence at his house? She opened his door with her hair wet. The thought of them together in his room the same way he was with me diminishes everything he said to me. Makes it all meaningless.

When the sun is high in the sky, painting colors across my room in purples and pinks, I hear footsteps, and then my bedroom door opens.

"Happy birthday, sweetheart," my mom says cheerfully.

I KEEP TRYING ARI, but her phone goes straight to voicemail. It's been a whole day since she's answered.

I keep pacing back and forth.

Julia showed up last night, begging me to let her in. She said the sewer backed up in her house, and she needed a place to shower. She couldn't ask anyone else. I didn't want to be a dick and tell her to go to a hotel. I was tempted to give her money so she could leave, but she whined and begged me she would be quick.

Javier was going out but promised to wait until she left. He said he was going to his room to get dressed, and I disappeared to my room, hoping it would encourage her to leave faster.

Javier has a grim expression on his face. I pinch my brows together and pull out my phone.

Rey: What's wrong?

Javier: Check the cameras.

I open my home security app and pull last night's feed, and my stomach drops. My insides clench in fear. I see Ari pull in and notice Julia's car. She walks up, Julia opens the door, and they exchange words.

I pause the recording, zoom in, and see the expression on Ari's face. No, baby. I wouldn't. I would never do that to you.

I look up from my phone. "You need to find her," Javier signs.

"She isn't answering my calls."

"Go to her. Explain that it wasn't what she thought."

I nod and grab my keys to head over to her apartment.

After an hour, I head back to the house and plop myself on the couch with my head in my hands. I'm fucking defeated because she isn't home. Her car was gone, and I waited in the parking lot.

If something happened to her, I don't think I could forgive myself.

Javier nudges my shoulder. I glance up, shake my head, and sign, "She wasn't home."

I'm angry and disappointed. Who knows what Julia said to her, but I plan on finding out.

Rey: What did you say to Ari last night?

Julia: I didn't say anything.

Rey: Don't play games, Julia. I saw you both on the security camera. You opened the door to my house.

Julia: When she drove up, I noticed the lights flashing and knew someone was at the door. I told her that you were in the shower and that I was in your bedroom. I explained to her that we have known each other for a long time, and that we always come back to each other.

Rey: Translation. You made it seem like we were fucking.

Julia: We have been fucking, Rey, for years. She is a woman you have just met.

My nostrils flare. I can't stand her, and I don't ever want to see her again.

> Rey: You have let the woman I love think the worst of me, Julia. I will never forgive you for this. You have crossed a line, and there is no coming back. I told you I don't love you, and I meant it. I don't. Never talk to me again or go near her spilling lies. We are done as friends. I don't want to see you ever again.

> Julia: Fine, Rey. You deserve it. You hurt me, and you deserve the same fate. To be alone.

I walk over to the kitchen, and Javier is sitting on the couch watching TV. He looks up at me, and I sign, "Julia made it seem that we were screwing when Ari showed up. If Julia shows up..."

"I'll throw her out."

"I don't know where Ari is, and she won't answer my calls."

REV

ON MONDAY AFTERNOON, I sigh in relief when I see Ari come through the door toward the office. Her hair is up in a messy bun; she looks tired but, at the same time, beautiful.

She closes the door when she sees me approach, and I open it and close it behind me, locking us both inside.

"We need to talk, Ari. It wasn't what—"

"I had sex with someone else," she signs, and she looks back down at her desk.

My chest rises and falls, and I begin to sweat. I feel like crumpling to the floor.

I shake my head because I must have misunderstood. "Ari."

She looks up, tears stream down her cheeks, and I'm crumbling. I'm breaking.

"I had sex with someone else. I'm just good enough to string along and fuck with on occasion. I get it. So save it. There is nothing to explain. I showed up to your house and, like Jimmy, you were in the shower fucking someone else. So, I fucked someone else. We're even. You can go now," she signs and then shoos me out of the office like I'm a dog.

She thought I was screwing Julia while being with her, and in her mind, I was no better than Jimmy, so she did something to wipe the hurt that she was feeling.

Picturing her with someone else feels like agony.

Another man kissing her, moving inside her while he heard her moans and cries of pleasure.

I sniff.

She looks up, and I can swear I see her frown, but then her lips form a thin line, and her eyes grow cold and lifeless. She is done with me. But I'm not going without a fight. I know Ari loves me, and deep down, I don't believe she did it. I don't believe she let someone else touch her.

I slam my hand on the desk in frustration, and she jumps. Her eyes grow wide. She throws a pen at me, and I duck. She grabs an eraser and aims it at my head. It misses me by an inch, and my eyes tell her what my words don't.

Run.

She gets up, lifts her chin defiantly, and walks over to me, full of anger and hurt in her eyes. She pushes me with her finger and then opens her palms flat and shoves against my chest. She says she hates me.

I can read her lips as she repeats the words over and over.

I move to grab her, but she steps back out of my reach, runs to the door, opens it, and runs out.

I don't care if we cause a scene. I don't care if everyone in the gym sees me run out after her.

I follow her until she reaches the locker room shower. I'm relieved that no one was inside changing, but she's not thinking right now.

I text Javier quickly, telling him to make sure no one comes into the locker room until I give him the okay.

I walk in and notice the lights are on the corner by the showers. I remove my shirt and place my phone on the bench to keep it from getting wet.

I walk over to the corner shower and see the water running. I walk past each divider until I reach Ari under the spray, crying.

Sobs wrack her body as her chest heaves, and I hate myself. I hate that she doesn't trust me. I hate that Julia lied to her, and it broke her. She saw Julia kiss me at the club. Ari thinks there is a possibility I want Julia when there is only her.

I move forward, trying not to get my sneakers wet. She is getting soaked under the spray, and I don't think she cares right now. I remove my shoes and socks, so I'm left in only my shorts.

Fuck it, I walk under the spray of warm water. I tilt her head by placing my finger under her chin, and she turns her face away. I grab her more forcefully against me by her arms.

She looks up, squinting against the spray.

I'm not gripping her hard enough to hurt her.

I would never hurt her.

"I didn't... sleep with her... after... you," I say, struggling to get the next words out. "Who was... it, Ari? Who?"

She shakes her head, and I look up, praying for a miracle. I don't want her to leave me, but I need to know who it was.

I release her and sign, "I didn't sleep with her. She lied."

I would never cheat on her. We're together.

She shakes her head, looks up, and signs, "I lied. I didn't sleep with anyone. I was hurt. It was my birthday, and I went to my parents for the weekend. I said that to hurt you the way you hurt me. I didn't think you even cared."

I kiss her forehead, relieved that she didn't sleep with anyone. It was her birthday, and I didn't think to check. I didn't plan something special for her.

I step back and remove her shirt.

I push her leggings down and peel them off her legs, dropping them on the floor. She is left in only her bra and thong. I turn her around and place her hands on the tiles with her palms facing flat.

I slide her hair to the side to access her ear. I lean close.

"Hold on, Ari. I need to have you right now. So you never question…" I take a deep breath. "How much I love you, baby." I press my lips on her neck and rasp, "*Eres mia.*"

I slip her panties to the side, and I slide the head of my cock at her entrance and shove into her so hard her feet almost lift off the floor. She braces herself for the onslaught of me thrusting deep inside her by holding herself steady with her hands on the tile.

I pull out and groan when I slide in again. I can feel the vibrations coming out of my throat.

Her head tilts back, and I kiss her shoulder.

"Mine," I growl.

I grip her hips and begin thrusting into her as deep as I can go, over and over. I take her hard.

Ari is it for me. Right now, this is me loving her. This is me showing her there is no way there will ever be anyone else except her.

I wrap my arm around her hips while I'm thrusting inside her and slide my fingers over her lower, holding her still.

I push up into her, faster and faster.

She falls against my chest as I'm going at it, pumping into her. Her tits bop up and down.

Whatever she wants, I'll give it to her.

I can feel her tense when she is about to come. I plunge into her deep as her orgasm rips through her.

The familiar tingle is at the base of my spine, and my balls draw up. I pump into her one last time, spilling my cum inside her.

Her chest heaves like she ran a marathon. The only marathon she ran was riding my cock.

When I slide out of her, she is tired, and her eyes are heavy. I pick her up and carry her so I can get a warm towel to wrap her body in. Her panties and bra are still on, but I will remove them once I can find her some warm clothes to change into.

I know I can get one of the gym T-shirts from the office, but I have to find a pair of my pants in my gym bag. I set her down on the bench and get another towel to wrap her hair in.

When I'm about to leave, she pulls me close so that my eyes are level with her lips. She knows I can't hear her, so she mouths what she wants to say to me so I can read her lips. "Next time, fuck me harder."

My mouth curls into a smile. Baby, I'm going to fuck you so hard every chance I get.

ARI

I DIDN'T KNOW how long I could keep up the lie. I didn't sleep with anyone this past weekend. How could I? All I could think about was how much I loved him. My parents cooked me breakfast and took me to dinner. All the while, my heart was disintegrating.

I wrote his name on a piece of paper and drew horns like he was Satan, but I still loved the devil. In my mind, he wasn't a saint, but my heart was bleeding.

When he told me in the shower right before he fucked me into oblivion that he didn't sleep with her, it was like an angel answered my prayers. I don't know what she was doing at his house, but I want to find out.

I got up from the couch Rey placed me on when he drove us over to his house in my car.

Javier is in the kitchen, and I make a cup of coffee. He turns and smiles when he sees me open the coffee maker.

"Are you okay?"

I smile. "I think so. Why?"

He raises his hands. "I'm just asking. He needed to carry you after you disappeared in the locker room, and I figured he must have tired you out."

"What if I slipped and fell?" I ask sarcastically with a light tease in my tone.

"There is only one thing you could have fallen...on. One thing that would make you both moan like you were filming a porno that echoed throughout the gym." My cheeks are on fire, and he can see I'm embarrassed, but he continues. "The fact that he had to carry you out wearing different clothes, and when you walked out... I hate to say it, but you walked funny to the car."

I burst out laughing. "I was not," I say defensively. "Oh, yes. You were," he says with a laugh.

I place my hands over my cheeks and drop my eyes to the coffee as it fills the cup.

"She lied to you." My eyes meet his, and I stay quiet, listening to what that bitch Julia lied about. "She showed up begging to use the shower because the sewer in her house was supposedly backed up. I'm not an expert, but that is what she said. Rey didn't want to let her in and told me to make sure she showered and left. He left for his room, and I didn't stay to watch her leave. When Rey couldn't reach you, something told me to check the camera, which is how we knew you showed up. Julia said something that upset you and made you think the worst."

"She's a bitch."

"Yeah, I don't think she can accept that Rey is in love with you. He didn't touch her, Ari. He confronted her via text and told her to never set foot in our house and never speak to us again. I never thought my brother could love so hard."

My heart feels like it's hovering. "It's crazy how jealous and spiteful people can get when they don't get what they want. People are not objects." I look up at Javier. "I love Rey with everything that I am, Javier. I love him so much. I want to work out my trust issues. I want to trust him."

He nods. "I think you guys need to figure things out."

Rey walks into the kitchen after his shower. I wanted to join him, but I was recuperating on the couch from our locker room session.

He smiles at me and kisses my temple, and I want to melt against him.

We order in, and the three of us watch a movie, but we mute the sound so we can shoot the shit and eat in front of the TV.

We sign or send Rey a text. When he laughs, I stop and stare. I've never loved someone's laughter the way I love his.

I stayed the night, and after a warm bath, I fell asleep in his arms.

He woke me up with a protein shake and a smile. I know he can't make me breakfast because that is one of Rey's weaknesses. The kitchen. He sucks at it.

He motions for me to check my phone. I lean over and grab it from the nightstand.

> Rey: After school today, are you ready for your first lesson?

I pinch my brows in confusion because I don't know what he's talking about.

> Ari: First lesson for what?

> Rey: How to throw a punch.

I look up and take a sip of the shake he made me. It's chocolate peanut butter, and it tastes good.

He wants to teach me how to defend myself? After the whole thing with Jimmy and how he attacked me by pulling my hair, he's right. I don't know how to defend myself or throw a solid punch.

I can land one, but it hurts like a bitch.

I shrug my shoulders and nod, telling him that I want to. He smiles and signs, "I'll wait for you so I can take you to school."

ARI

AFTER SCHOOL, Rey picks me up, and we drive to my apartment so I can pick up workout clothes and some toiletries.

He smiles when I return and slide into my SUV's passenger side.

We head to the gym, and I look at the radio and wonder if he finds it rude of me to play music. He glances at me briefly and shakes his head. I think he saw me look at the screen.

He presses the music app, and music begins to play.

I smile, and I guess he doesn't seem to mind. I leave it on a dance station, filling the silence since he can't sign or text me while driving.

When he parks in his spot in front of the gym, he turns to me and signs, "I don't want you to sacrifice things because I can't hear."

"It is not a sacrifice when it comes to you. I don't want you to feel uncomfortable. I also don't want to be rude."

"I don't want you to feel like you have to treat me special or anything. I want to feel normal. And for the record, it doesn't make much of a difference if I can hear it."

I drop my gaze. He feels uncomfortable when I can't listen to music because he can't hear. I get it. He wants to feel normal, and I think I messed up by asking him.

"I can't hear it either way, Ari. It's stupid that you must sacrifice something you like because of me. It makes me feel bad, and I worry you will resent me one day."

"I'm sorry," I sign.

He reaches out and places his hands over mine. "Don't be sorry," he says, a little off pitch.

I lean close and place a soft kiss on his lips. When I pull back, I mouth, "Okay." He smiles, sliding from the driver's side to move around the car. He opens my door.

When I get settled in the office after an hour of finishing up and making sure all the money has been collected for the members this month, he motions to my clothes and then the locker room to go get changed.

When I get up and head out of the office, I notice he follows me when he sees my bag slung over my shoulder. He smiles when I go in and stays outside like my bodyguard in front of the door. He wants to make sure no one goes inside while I'm changing.

When I'm ready, I walk out, and his eyes widen.

I'm wearing windbreakers and a sports bra and no shirt. My hair is in a braid.

I watch as he bites his bottom lip. I place my thumb so his teeth can release it.

He holds my hand and walks me over to the punching bag. He stands behind me, and I wish I had thought of this sooner because I would have let Rey teach me anything when he stood this close to me. His hands are on my waist, and I feel the tingles on my skin.

Boxing is the most physically demanding sport, making it an excellent form of exercise. It requires quick reflexes, dexterity, strength, stamina, and mental fortitude. Okay, I read up online before he called me out to change.

Rey begins to show me how to stand and balance my power.

After fifteen minutes, my arms are on fire from holding them up. There is a science to it, a strategy, and you have to read your opponent.

The most essential aspect of boxing is opening doors you never knew existed within yourself. It pushes you on the inside.

Everyone has a hidden fighter; boxing is a great way to bring it out. That is what Rey is doing right now. He isn't just showing me how to throw a punch. He's showing me without words how to connect with my inner self, not only to defend myself, but also to find my strength and not be afraid.

I understand why he loves this sport. Rey had to learn to fight, be the best, and overcome life's obstacles. To never accept defeat. Coming from Puerto Rico to the States as a kid with his younger brother and a single mother was challenging. A challenge he faced. His mother learned to speak English, and since he was a young kid, he knew not only to box but also to use a whole new way to communicate. Body language, how to read people with his eyes, and how to read their expressions.

It is amazing, and I feel connected to him just by him taking the time to show me the way he sees things.

The way he fights is beautiful because he wants me to be part of him. He wants to share with me everything he loves and cares about. This is more than defending myself. This is Rey loving me and protecting me.

He trains me for the next hour and even Javier joins us.

"You're doing good. You look good. I'm surprised he hasn't thrown a sweater over you, but I think he is getting used to the idea that no matter what, guys in the gym will check you out. As long as it's respectable," he teases.

I lower my hands. They're burning from keeping them up to protect my face.

"Right now, I want to learn so I can punch them in the face when they do," I tease.

Javier smiles. "Atta, sis. You have the best teacher in the world. You'll be kicking ass and taking names in no time."

I keep hitting the bag hard, and my knuckles are beginning to get sore under the gloves. Rey stops me and frowns when he sees my knuckles are red after pulling off the gloves. He shakes his head in disappointment.

I look up after he places the Ziploc bag filled with ice on my hand, and he signs, "I'm buying you special gloves."

"Okay, as long as you teach me," I sign.

I enter the office and spot a box wrapped in wrapping paper with my name on it. I look over my shoulder, and Rey and Javier are picking up the equipment.

I pick up the box, and there is a card from Rey taped to it and says: Happy Birthday, Aria.

I didn't expect him to get me anything. I never anticipated another gift from him, especially after the stunning car he has already given me.

I untie the bow, the satin ribbon slipping through my fingers. In the box, resting on a plush black pillow, is a red origami swan—a nostalgic reminder of the first gift he ever gave me. Alongside it is a set of keys and a note.

Aria,

They told me I lost my hearing at twelve, but they were wrong. They didn't know that I was destined to hear only the rhythm of your heart when I found you. To reserve my words for you, for those moments when our foreheads touch, like the mute swans, when they mate for life. My love for you is a language that needs no sound, only the touch of our souls.

I wasn't sure what to give you for your birthday, but I wanted it to be something everlasting. Here are the keys to my home. Whenever you're feeling lonely or you need me, whenever you want someone to watch romance movies with or talk about anything, I'll be there. I'll be waiting for you to fall asleep in my arms, listening to the beating of our hearts.

I love you, Aria.

Always, Rey

ARI

EVERY DAY, for about an hour or two, after the other fighters have already left, he takes his time and walks me through scenarios of what to do when someone attacks.

He isn't showing me that I can overpower someone bigger than me, but he is showing me how to be smart, use my mind to my advantage, spot someone's weakness, and defend myself.

Every day, I learn something new. I learn something different.

I don't sleep in Rey's house every night despite the heartfelt note he gave me as a birthday present. Because he gave me a raise, I bought a more comfortable bed.

I try to stay in my apartment at least twice weekly because I still want independence. I need time to think about what I want, even if a man promises the world. I have to eliminate doubt and insecurities.

Rey never asked me to leave and get my own place, but I couldn't stay and take advantage. I needed to know that I could take care of myself.

———

I'm in the office catching up on some paperwork. Chase strolls in after I've sent out the bill payments and knocks on the door to get my attention.

I look up, and I smile. "Hey, Chase, how's it going?"

"I miss seeing you around. I always find you in here or out there," he says brightly. "You look good. He takes his time with you. I think the guys are jealous. He doesn't push on your shoulder to get your attention or snort when you fuck up."

I laugh through my nose and say, "I'm learning for different reasons than what you guys come here for. He is teaching me to defend myself if he isn't around to save me."

I look through the window; Rey is watching me. I give him a reassuring wave.

Chase looks behind me and then at me. "Should I go before he comes in here like a caveman?"

I laugh. "You don't have to, but maybe I'll go over there."

"I think you should, Ari, or I'll be on the speed bag for a week straight."

I give him a grin. "He wouldn't."

He snorts. "For you, there is nothing he wouldn't do."

I walk over to where Rey is in the corner by the bell. Two fighters are in the middle of the ring and have just finished sparring. He turns his head when he spots me walking over and gives me a panty-melting smile.

I reach over when Chase catches up and give him a fist bump.

Rey smiles at me. I give him one hand, then the other so he can pull me up. I wrap my arms around him. He bends and presses our foreheads together. Our noses touch. He looks at me like I'm the fire to his soul. The symphony to his heart.

I would never leave him.

I could never abandon him.

But I need time, like a flower in the garden waiting to bloom to become something beautiful.

ARI

IT'S THURSDAY NIGHT, and I'm out getting something to eat. Rey had wanted me to stay over, but I'd never get my studying done. I'll be too busy on him or under him. Every time I'm in bed with him, I want to explore every inch of his hard body.

I enter a local college spot to pick up the food. I don't feel like cooking because I have a term paper due, and I'm halfway done.

I'm standing in line when I notice a lot of people with Flyers T-shirts and hats.

I look through the take-out window. The place has wood paneling, with dollar bills stuck on the wood. There are signatures of students who have come through over the years. Some have gone pro. People cheer while watching TV and drinking beer. I walk down the bar. College students wearing Flyers jerseys and T-shirts line up at the bar to order drinks.

Dread crawls down my spine because I hope it means people are just watching a game on TV.

This place serves good food, is cheap, and is also a sports bar where students hang out to drink and watch the games.

Since breaking up with Jimmy, I haven't watched a single hockey game. I don't even know what their schedule is.

I hear shouting in the back. Guys are chanting for some girls to take shots.

I'm sure it's their way to get the girls shit-faced so they can get a quick bang on a Thursday night.

Why do girls fall for that? But then again, some girls don't even care. They'll do anything to sleep with a guy if he's hot, especially for free shots.

"Oh my God, it is you." I hear a girl say to my right.

I turn while waiting in the ridiculous line to pick up my food. Why is the line long when my food is supposed to be ready? It is takeout for a reason and the point of ordering it by phone beforehand. Sometimes I don't understand restaurants, but this is better than a greasy fast food burger that will give me a stomachache in the morning.

"It is," the girl to my right says.

"Are you talking to me?" I ask.

"Oh yeah, I'm sorry. My name is Ginger." She picks up a strand of her hair to show me how she got her name.

"I wouldn't have guessed."

"I'm sorry, but you have been all over social media since you started dating the hot-ass boxer Rey Vicente. I noticed it was you because his brother always posts pictures of you guys training. It is so cute that he is teaching you how to box. There are also people posting that you used to be in a serious relationship with Jimmy Harding."

I notice she is with a group of friends, and they all have drinks in their hands.

One of them smiles at me. "You have to tell us your secret."

"Secret?"

"Yeah, how did you land two rich athletes?"

I scratch the top of my head, trying to figure out why girls are this shallow and ask stupid questions. There is no secret.

"It sure isn't drinking at a bar. I met Rey through his brother and Jimmy when he attended Penn State before he went pro. Which means when he was broke."

They all look at each other, and I know whatever I said flew over their heads, but at least I tried.

The crowd parts, and the last person I want to see walks through.

Shit. Jimmy.

If the universe could swallow me whole, I would love for it to happen right now so I can escape.

I look away before he spots me, but when I glance over, he is looking at me appreciatively. He motions to one of his teammates with the neck of his beer and tells him something.

His friend looks over at me and winks. I roll my eyes.

The restraining order was temporary, and I didn't have enough evidence to prove he was a danger to my life to make it permanent, so the judge dropped it.

The line begins to move faster, and the group of girls moves to the other side of the bar. I open my phone and the social media app to see what they are talking about. I click on Rey's profile, and there are cute pictures of Rey and me at the gym. There are good shots of him teaching me and others where he is right behind me and is standing closer than necessary. There is even one where he is kissing my head.

"Your smile is still beautiful, Ari." My head snaps up when I heard Jimmy's voice.

"Jimmy, you—"

He raises his hands. "I know. I just can't help but say that I still love you."

I shake my head, annoyed that he still doesn't get it. Jimmy's problem isn't that he loves me. He doesn't like to lose.

He steps back. His friends smirk like they were in on a secret I was unaware of. I grab my food and pay for it, trying to get out of there as fast as I can.

I unlock my car, get in, and lock the doors. I back out and head home.

I text Rey when I make it home.

> Ari: I made it home. When I was getting my
> food, I ran into Jimmy.

> Rey: Shit, Ari. Did he say anything to you?

> Ari: Yeah, he came up with his friends and
> said he still loved me, but I warned him. He
> backed off, and I'm home.

> Rey: Tell me if you need me to come and
> get you.

I get out of my car and lock it, walking up the stairway to the second floor. I'm about to close the door when it is quickly shoved open, causing me to fall back and drop my food.

When I look up, Jimmy smiles at me like a predator that has his prey cornered right where he wants them.

"Hello, Ari." He leans close after he shuts the door and flicks the locks. "I've missed you. I'm glad you invited me to hang out like old times." I want to puke when I smell the beer on his breath. Rey was right. Jimmy needs mental help.

He grabs my hair, pain shooting in the back of my skull. And drags me toward the bedroom. "Ahh, stop it. You're hurting me, Jimmy."

He releases my hair when he shoves me on the bed. I get up and throw a punch to his jaw.

His head rears back, and then he laughs.

"You have been dying to hit me since you found out I was fucking Mandy in the shower. I even liked the way you got all mad because she was riding my dick. But here is the thing." He leans close, pinning me on the bed. I struggle. He is bigger and stronger. I try to lift my left leg to kick him, but he pushes me into the mattress. His body is over me, and I try to kick, shove, scratch, but he pins me.

"She likes it when I have sex with you, and she cleans me off. She likes it, Ari. She likes the idea of me and you and her on the side."

"You're sick," I say through clenched teeth.

"You were always the first, baby." He rubs his hard cock into me, and I want to gag. "This is what you do to me, Ari. I get so hard for you."

"Get off me! HELP! HELP!" I scream.

I'm tired from fighting, and I know he is going to rape me.

I play possum. When he releases my hands, I rear my fist back and punch him in the face.

"You bitch!" He yells in pain, placing his hands over his face.

I scramble from the bed and run to the front door.

The door swings open, and Rey appears. Tears run down my cheeks. He came.

He takes one look at me, and he knows. He can tell that something is wrong.

Jimmy leaves the room with a bloody nose, and Rey doesn't waste time. He gets in a fighter stance and hits Jimmy with an uppercut.

Jimmy falls back with a thud against the wall. I grab my phone and dial 911.

"Nine one one, what is your emergency?" the operator says through the phone.

I tell them what happened in a shaky voice, looking at Jimmy out cold on the floor.

Rey wraps me in his arms. I'm trembling. "Did he, Ari? Did he?"

I know what he is asking, and I shake my head, and he sighs in relief.

We wait until the cops show up, and I'm grateful Jimmy is still out cold. The cops come and arrest him, and he's going to jail. Rey says he will take care of everything and that I landed an excellent punch.

> Rey: You did good, baby. I'm proud of you.
>
> Ari: How did you know?
>
> Rey: I felt it the day he touched you. I had a bad feeling he wouldn't let it go, but I had to be sure. That is why I wanted to take you to school and not let you out of my sight.
>
> Ari: Thank you, Rey.
>
> Rey: I'll feel better if you stay with me.

I look up and nod.

I grabbed enough clothes to stay with Rey for a while. He helped lock up the apartment and throw away anything that could perish.

I didn't want to involve my parents, but I had to call them so they knew I was okay.

It was quickly all over the news about Jimmy and how Rey came just in time to save me from what Jimmy planned. He was immediately suspended from the Flyers and soon dropped from pro hockey.

Rey texted his lawyer, and I immediately agreed to press charges.

It also meant that I wasn't leaving The Sweat Box. I couldn't leave Rey.

Rey and Javier were like two guardian angels. It is scary to think of the situation I put myself in getting involved with Jimmy.

What Jimmy revealed to me in my apartment made me realize that I was living with a person who was not right mentally.

Rey sent one of his friends to pick up his car from my apartment and drop it off at his house.

When we arrive, Javier is waiting for us. He walks up to the car, and he gets my bags.

"Hey, *Hermanita*. Are you okay? I'm glad Rey was there."

I give him a smile. "Yeah." I look up when Rey goes and gets my suitcase out of the back. "My badass boyfriend came just in time to kick his ass and save me."

Javier turns around and looks at Rey, waiting for me to come inside and sign what I just said.

Rey gives me a sexy smile and a wink. "Always. I promised...you. I would never let anyone hurt you, Ari," he says with so much emotion.

His voice is the best sound in the world.

I run up to him and wrap my hands around his neck. "I love you," I mouth, reaching up, and he bends so I can press my lips to his.

ARI

IT'S FRIDAY, and we are heading up to meet my parents. I'm nervous. They had called me so they could finally meet my boyfriend, the man who saved me. My parents were upset I didn't fill them in on my birthday weekend when I showed up at night moping around the house, giving them two-word answers.

They probably figured it was because I was dealing with psycho Jimmy and not thinking the worst about Rey with Julia.

He pulls into the driveway, my parents anxiously waiting on the small porch.

My mother's eyes widen when she spots Rey. "Jesus," my mother mutters.

Rey is a big man and good-looking.

She gives me a thumbs-up when no one is looking.

Rey is kind, and even though he looks intimidating, there is a heart of gold under all his muscles.

My father's eyes water, and he shakes Rey's hand for saving his daughter.

I fan myself to keep from crying because my parents love Rey.

I told them he was deaf, but it was like I hadn't told them. I could see the excitement in my parents' eyes. They had boxing royalty in their presence. The world thinks he has some hearing loss due to fighting, but they don't know the truth. They don't know that he is a legend and has defied all odds.

He's proved to the world that he would make it. Even though life throws you a curveball, you figure out how to smack it out of the park. Rey took the world in silence. He stole my heart with his words and the beat with his heart.

When I follow my parents inside, they offer him a seat. He nods politely and sits on the small couch. I take a seat facing him—close enough to touch but far enough to sign.

"Honey, where are you staying now?"

I swallow and sign so Rey knows what my mother asks me. He gives me a slight nod to tell them.

I clear my throat. "I have my own apartment. I work at Rey's boxing gym, but under the circumstances, I'm staying with Rey at his home."

My mother's eyes widened, and she asked, "Sweetheart, who bought you that very expensive car? We know you can't afford it."

I take a deep breath and smile at Rey. My parents are nosy and can be overprotective.

"Rey, Mom. My car gave up on me, and Rey wanted to make sure I was..."

"Safe," she finishes for me. "I can see that."

My father looks up at Rey and says slowly, "Thank you for taking care of our little girl."

Rey nods and glances at me. "My...pleasure," he says slowly, the words clear and even. The sound makes my heart beat wildly. It's like he can hear it.

REY

IT'S BEEN a month since the incident with Jimmy, and the anticipation for the special date I've planned in the backyard for Ari is building up.

We spend most of our time together, but we've agreed to take things slow.

I respect Ari's independence, which is why she still has her apartment that I furnished as a gift even though she practically lives in my house.

But she has the option to go to her apartment whenever she wants.

Right now, she needs that safety net—the security of her own place—in case something goes wrong with us. It won't, but she's been hurt before, and if I can make her feel safe, secure, and loved, that's all that matters.

Someday, she won't need that apartment anymore. She will trust me and have enough trust in us, but until then, it is worth every penny.

News got out on social media about what happened between Jimmy and me over Ari. Our relationship has been dubbed a love story.

"Everything is all set," Javier signs.

I have set up a giant screen to play *The Notebook*. I had a company come out and install the huge projector screen and shovel the snow. Heaters dot the area, and I have a fire pit to keep us warm. I had a daybed placed in front of the screen so we could watch her favorite movie play as we ate s'mores and popcorn. I can't hear it, but we will have the subtitles scrolling. The fact that I'm with Ari is enough to make this a perfect night. I've watched the movie plenty of times to know what comes next. I'm not Noah, but I'm her Rey.

The tiny black box is hidden in my pocket, and I'm hoping she will say yes. My nerves are everywhere, but I'm confident. Even if she says no, I'm okay with that. I'll keep trying to be what she needs until she feels the time is right. The anticipation is overwhelming, but it's a feeling I wouldn't trade for anything.

I check my phone after it vibrates. I wave the phone up, motioning to Javier. He looks up after making sure the sound is working, and after a minute, he gives me a thumbs-up.

Ari: I'm here. Where are you guys?

Rey: In the backyard.

Ari: Okay, I'm coming. I'll be right out.

ARI

REY TOLD me he had a special night in mind, but I wasn't sure if we were going out. He said to dress warm, so I'm wearing flat over-the-knee boots, wool leggings, a long sweater with gloves, and a hat.

When I walk out to the backyard, I gasp, the cold mist escaping my lips. Lights are strewn across the backyard, giving it an intimate glow. There is a daybed in front of a gigantic projector screen. He had the backyard turned into a movie night. There is a firepit with platters of food, buckets of popcorn, and a bottle of wine chilling in a bucket of ice—all for me.

I can't help it. I start crying. Tears of happiness flow down my cheeks at how beautiful it looks and that he went all out for our date night. I have never had anyone do something like this for me. It's special, and I can't help but fall more in love with Rey. The past weeks have been the best in my life. I'm so happy Christmas is almost here. I have one of the best gifts, Rey, but I also have something I need to tell him besides how much I love him.

I can tell he thought about this and planned it. He has been wonderful since that day with Jimmy. We are officially together, but he's letting me set the pace for our relationship. I've stayed mostly at his house but kept the apartment, and he understood why. He doesn't pressure me, and I don't pressure him.

We have been working more on expressing our love for each other. He has shown me how much he loves me ever since the night I made Javier his soup, which I still think was a setup, but Javier emphatically denies it.

Javier greets me. "Hey, Ari. I hope you like it. He's been planning this for quite a while."

"It looks beautiful."

Rey walks over and opens his hands wide. He is wearing a jacket over his designer sweatpants and hoodie.

"I love it," I sign.

"I love you, Ari. I will try every day to show you how much."

I fan myself to keep from crying harder. "I love you, too."

"I'll leave you guys to it," Javier says and signs as he walks back inside the house.

I walk up to Rey and look up into his eyes. "I love you," I say slowly so he can read my lips.

We have been working on communicating this way. He reads my lips, and he speaks instead of texting all the time or using ASL.

"I love you more," he says.

He presses play, and it's my favorite movie, *The Notebook*. It begins to play, and he motions for us to lie down on the daybed, lifting a fuzzy white blanket that looks like fur, but I know it's faux fur.

We eat and watch the movie, but it feels off and is different. I press mute on the remote and read the subtitles along with him.

"Why did you mute it?" he whispers after the mute sign appears on the screen.

I sit up, turn to him, and sign so he can understand. "I want to watch it the same way you watch it."

He slides his thumb over the pulse beating on my throat and closes his eyes. I lean forward and kiss his lips softly, my forehead resting against his.

He hands me a note and nods for me to open and read it.

Ari,

I thought I lost part of my life when I lost the ability to hear. I began to live and accept the world in silence. Only bits and pieces were given to me, with the rest slowly being taken away. But as time passed, the sounds slowly faded into a few scattered notes. Even if the volume is so loud, I can hardly hear a sound; sometimes it's the sound of whispers or beats. I play the recordings you left me because I only want to remember hearing you. I want it to be to the sound of your voice, even if it's a whisper. When I can't hear at all, the memory of the sound of my name on your lips will be imprinted on my heart and soul. How you look at me is enough to tell me you love me. I will always be able to see and feel what I can't hear. It is what I will take with me forever.

It is the only thing that matters. I don't need to write you love letters for a year to tell you how much I love you. The feeling of our hearts beating together for each other is the greatest sound in the world. Nothing is more beautiful than that. I don't need to build you a house to show you I love you because wherever you are, that is my home.

When I told you the first time to never leave me, I whispered words I had never said to anyone. I didn't realize it at first, but my heart and soul recognized it as my soulmate. This time, I'm going to tell you I will never leave you because you and I are one.

I don't need to hear when I have you. You make me whole. I don't feel like I've lost anything. I'm going to ask you this because I'm ready. If you aren't, that is okay. I'll wait. I'm sure of you, and I'm sure of us.

Someone special once told me that the greatest love story is never written; it is lived. This is our story—the one we live, the one no one can read about because this one is ours, and there will be no other like it.

I'm ready, Ari. I'll always love you. I want to have babies—lots of babies with you. I want our home filled with love because we have so much to give our children.

You're my forever.
WILL YOU MARRY ME?

I look up and place my hand over my heart. It is beating so fast.

Rey is holding a black box in his hand with a hopeful smile.

I can't describe my feelings because there is so much emotion. My eyes blur, and all I see are the bright lights. I look around and take it all in. I want to remember this moment forever.

He flips the velvet box open, and the most gorgeous ring sparkles in the twinkling light.

I nod and say slowly, "Yes! A thousand times, yes."

He slides the ring on my finger, and I wrap my arms around his neck. Our phones ding and vibrate. I look down, and he points at my phone.

I open the social media app notification, and it shows a picture of us just a minute ago when I said yes. He then slid the ring on my finger.

Javier must have been hiding somewhere to take the picture.

It reads, The Future Mrs. Vicente. #Shesaidyes #Myforever #ReyandAri

I glance up from my phone, his eyes meet mine, and I sign, "I have something to tell you."

"Okay," he signs.

I drop my eyes, and with my hands, I sign, "I'm pregnant."

When I look up, tears run down his cheeks. He drops to his knees and places his ear on my stomach. I know I'm only seven weeks along, but he is already dying to feel the baby. He wants to hear the baby with his hands, cheek, and skin. He presses soft kisses to my flat stomach. Last month, he said he wanted to start a family before it was too late and he couldn't hear at all.

My fingers run through his hair. He looks up at me, and his eyes light up.

"I'm gonna be an uncle?" he asks with a big smile and his phone in hand.

I nod, and he snaps another picture of Rey on his knees and his face on my stomach.

My phone dings with an alert. I look at my phone, and we are all tagged.

She's pregnant! #babyvicenteontheway #Imabeanuncle

I look up. "Hey, brother?"

"Yeah, *Hermanita*."

"Where is your girlfriend?" I ask.

He shrugs, and his eyes dim. "When she shows up like you did for my brother."

The End.

Want to read my next release? Pre-order Sugar Coated Secrets with the link below.

SUGAR COATED SECRETS

If you want to read something darker? Get a head start with the prequels to Lover's Fate, a new collection of dark books coming October 24th 2024.

Carmen Rosales
Writing as
Delilah Croww

HORROR X

Whispers in the Dark (Alice)
Circle of Freaks by Delilah Croww (Ivy)
Lover's Fate Book One preorder

About the Author

Carmen Rosales is a best-selling dark romance and Latinx author. She loves to write in different genres of Romance. She also writes gothic horror under her alter ego, Delilah Croww. Beyond her writing, Carmen is a devoted wife and mother who loves spending time with her loved ones.

Join her VIP list and visit her shop at www.carmenros ales.com